I0519948

Tales: The Benevolence Archives, Vol. 3 is a work of fiction.

LUTHER M. SILER

TALES:

THE BENEVOLENCE ARCHIVES
VOL. 3

PROSTETNIC
PUBLICATIONS

Dedicated to Corrie

The coolest neatest awesomest and bestest person
ever

Because shut up, that's why

TABLE OF CONTENTS

FOREWORD

This one was rough, folks.

Tales: The Benevolence Archives, Vol. 3, formerly known as *Tales from the Benevolence Archives: Volume 3 of the Benevolence Archives* until I realized how insanely unwieldy that title was, is my sixth book. Six! It is completely ridiculous to me that I've released six books, even if two of them are properly novellas. The thing is, *Tales* was originally *Sunlight,* which was the sequel to *Skylights* ... which is not a *Benevolence Archives* book. Then that book fell apart on the page on me as I realized that I was telling the wrong story. I picked *Tales* up, knowing that I had seeds for several stories in my head already, thinking *Oh, we'll just knock this next BA book out, then, it'll be easy.*

That was in March of 2016. I had managed a nice little two-books-a-year pace before that. And in the post where I let everyone know I was putting *Sunlight* on hold, I gave everyone a target date for *Tales:* June of 2016.

I'll wait while you laugh at me. It's okay. *I'm* laughing at me.

Let's just say I've blown a *lot* of deadlines since then, and that one wonderful thing about being an independent author is that when you have a year that, to be *charitable*, has more than its usual share of personal and political and societal dramatics and trouble, when you blow your deadlines you have no one who can *fire* you. You have fans you can disappoint— or at least one *hopes* one has fans— but they have all been wonderful and supportive and I don't think anyone has kicked me off of their bookshelves for being late just yet.

That said, I like how it turned out: eight new stories, some of which make our universe a bit bigger, some of which push the story forward, and one set in the earliest days of our heroes as a team. There's a couple of clues here and there about where the series is heading next, too— and the next *Benevolence Archives* book will be another full-length novel. I may do another short story collection after that, but Vol. 4 will be one coherent story.

Some thank-yous: Thanks to Matt Davis for naming Del Kormus from *The Duel*, winning what I framed as a contest on Twitter but was actually a complete inability to brain. Thanks to Jamie Noble Frier for the *outstanding* cover, the first time our heroes have actually appeared on a *Benevolence Archives* cover. My favorite part? *Brazel's clothes.* Thanks to Real Authors Michael J. Martinez and Anne Leonard for being kind enough to provide cover blurbs, even if both of them are technically for *BA* vol. 1. And thanks, as always, to my family and most especially to my wife Becky for putting up with me while I kvetched and complained and wrote three sentences and called that a day and then took another week before I wrote another word.

The next book will be faster. No, really. I *promise*.

Yours,

Luther M. Siler
Somewhere in Northern Indiana
September 8, 2017

THE DUEL

"*Checkmate,*" Grond said, sliding a knight into position. The pale human on the other side of the table glared at the chessboard for a moment, then sighed and surrendered her king, laying the piece on its side. "Congratulations," she said, offering a hand across the table. Grond took it, taking care not to squeeze too hard, as her hand was like a child's compared to his. The lights came up in the room, and the chess pieces on the table flickered and disappeared as the crowd surrounding them began to clap and cheer.

There was a barely audible hum as the public address system cut in. YOUR WINNER, NOW THE THREE-TIME WINNER OF THE PERRETON DISTRICT CHESS CHAMPIONSHIP, the voice intoned, GROND

OF ARRADON! Grond raised a hand over his head, waving to the crowd, and adjusted his glasses. He generally only wore them as an affectation while reading, but had found that they also tended to be slightly distracting to opponents during chess matches as well. It was difficult enough to play chess against a halfogre. His opponents tended to worry that he would lose his temper if he lost, which occasionally led to them making silly mistakes. Playing chess against a halfogre in business attire and *glasses* was more than a lot of them could handle.

Not that that had helped him against this opponent. His runner-up, whose name was Del, was a fine competitor, and he'd lost as many matches against her as he'd won over the last few years. He lifted her hand over her head as well and gestured for the crowd to continue cheering. The announcer took the hint. AND YOUR RUNNER-UP, DEL KORMUS OF ELDRAVVAR!

"Where's Eldravvar?" he whispered. "And last I checked your last name wasn't Kormus."

"I made it up," she said, a grin on her face. "Had somebody try to follow me home from one of these things once. I didn't want to have to blow anyone up after this tournament."

Grond shrugged. "Might make up for losing the purse," he said.

"You could always just give me your prize money," Del answered.

The halfogre grinned broadly. "I'll buy you dinner next time we do this," he said. "We'll call it even."

"Done," she answered.

*   *   *

The comm light was blinking when he got back to his rented room a few minutes later.

"Play," he said.

It was Rhundi. "Grond, it's me. Got something for you. Get back with me."

Grond chuckled and opened a comm channel.

"Congratulations," Rhundi said.

"About what?" he asked.

"You won the tournament," she said.

"I won *fifteen minutes ago*," he said. "How did you-"

"Grond. It's *me*," she said.

He stopped protesting.

"And I see you beat Del again. That's two in a row. You should start trying tournaments with a higher level of competition."

"The Risik Invitational won't let me in anymore, remember?" he said. "That'd be the next step up."

"Oh, right," she said. "Have I apologized for that lately?"

"Yes, to *me*," he said. "*They're* still mad."

Rhundi ignored this.

"So, listen. I know you're on vacation, but something just came across my desk and I thought you might be interested."

"You've got a job?"

"No. *Prescott* has a job. And he actually asked for you specifically. And since you were already on Carocawa—"

"Prescott's on Carocawa?"

"Yep."

"What's the job?"

"He didn't say. Just said he had something for you

and was wondering if I would, his words, 'loan you to him' for a few days."

Grond bristled. He'd been property in the past. He didn't especially like being treated like a *thing*.

Rhundi noticed the silence. "I don't think that's what he meant, Grond."

"Of course he did," Grond said. "Prescott's a dick. But his money spends. He really didn't tell you the job?"

"I figured since you were already nearby I'd just let you look into it. I didn't commit you. I just said I'd tell you about it."

"I'm told," he said. "And my price just went up fifteen percent. Dickery surcharge."

"Fine with me," she said. "I'll set up a meet for you tomorrow and comm you when and where."

"I just flew here in a planethopper," he reminded her. "If he wants me shooting at things I'll have to come home and resupply."

"I'll make sure he knows," she said. "Go out and do something fun. Extend your vacation by however long it takes to do this; I don't have much piling up over here yet."

"Whatever you say, boss," he said.

"One more thing," she said. "You ever met Prescott before?"

Grond thought about it. "No, actually," he said. "Done a handful of jobs for the guy but they all came through you."

Rhundi chuckled.

"He's got a thing," she said. "Don't look at it."

"A thing," Grond said.

"A thing."

"You wanna be a little bit more specific about this

thing?"

"Nah," she said. "Just that he doesn't like people drawing attention to it. So don't stare. Let me know how it goes, okay?"

"You're kidding—" he said, and she dropped the connection.

Shit, Grond thought.

*   *   *

Grond arrived at the meeting first, and was quietly amused at the near-panic his appearance created among the staff at the restaurant Prescott had selected, a place called Banik's in a surprisingly classy district. He'd expected somewhere much seedier, and was distinctly more shabbily-dressed than most of this place's mostly human clientele. A few dwarves and elves dotted the tables here and there, but he was the only being there of ogre extraction.

"You're gonna need to find me a bigger table," he said to the host. *Prescott did this on purpose*, he thought. Not to inconvenience him. This was directed at the restaurant. The owner had probably pissed Prescott off at some point.

Too bad I didn't come ready for a fight, he thought. He wasn't dressed for a chess match, but at least most of his tattoos were covered, and he was only wearing one or two easily noticeable weapons.

The host gulped, hurriedly saying something into an earpiece.

"We'll have your table in a moment, sir," he said, and Grond watched as a few dwarves muscled a larger table onto the dining room floor and brought out a chair more suited to his frame. Prescott was human; they'd have to bring out a higher chair for him as well, a thought that amused Grond to no end. It was difficult for ogres and humans to sit at the same bars and tables without at least one of them looking rather ridiculous. He considered insisting that the table be moved farther away from the kitchen and decided against it. Unless he was specifically told he was there to cause trouble, there was no point in it.

"Thanks," he said to the host, and went and sat down without being asked. A waiter quietly deposited a large glass of water in front of him and swiped at the table, which displayed a menu on its surface. Grond sorted the menu by price and ordered several of the most expensive items, only barely paying attention to what he was getting. He decided he was going to order something else every five minutes until Prescott showed up.

Luckily for his host, he only had to wait another four. Grond kept careful control of his facial muscles as Prescott arrived and climbed into the chair that had been set for him on the other side of the table. Climbed, because Prescott was easily one of the shortest human beings Grond had ever seen. In fact, only the human-looking ears and lack of a *snout* convinced Grond that he was actually looking at a human and not a gnome that had shaved off all its fur. His clothes were fine enough that he fit in with the rest of the restaurant's clientele, but he wore them with the air of a man who wasn't comfortable with what he was wearing and probably never would be.

The fact that he had the word "THIEF" embedded into his forehead, glowing bright blue— Grond suspected brightly enough to see by at night— didn't help with the ensemble any.

A nanotattoo. Grond had heard of them, but despite having spent a large amount of time in tattoo parlors had never actually seen one, since they were usually used by law enforcement on certain planets in Benevolence space for precisely this purpose— to mark criminals. The tattoo couldn't be covered up; it would simply glow more brightly if covered with makeup. If the bearer tried to cover it with something, it would either relocate itself to somewhere else on the body or simply separate itself from the skin and settle atop whatever the person was wearing. They were typically used for criminals who were actually *in* jail to guard against escape. The fact that Prescott's was still live and glowing implied that he'd broken out of prison and had never managed to get his deactivated.

I wonder if Irtuus-bon has a way around that, Grond thought. Rhundi's troll scientist had managed to penetrate the biolocking mechanisms on Benevolence guns. Surely he could find a way to remove a nanotattoo, especially for the right price.

"I already ordered," Grond said. "You want anything?"

Prescott brought up the menu and stared at it for a moment. "You must be hungry," he said.

"Nah," Grond answered. "I just want food."

Prescott shrugged and added something to the order.

"May as well cut to the chase," the little man said. His voice was deeper than Grond expected. "I need a second."

"You've got until I'm done eating, at least," Grond said.

Prescott looked confused for a moment, then winced.

"No, I mean ... shit, you know, a *second*. I need one. I don't know what else to call it. Somebody to fight on my behalf."

Grond very nearly spit some of his water across the table. "You mean you need a *champion*. You got challenged to a *duel?*"

"I did," he said. "Somebody trying to weasel out of some money he owed me. Human named Barron. You'd hate him. Real scummy guy. Decided to trump up some reason why I wasn't worthy of his money. Said it *impyooned his honor* to pay me. I told 'im to fuck himself and he threw a glove at me. A literal fuckin' glove." He blew his nose noisily on a napkin. "Guess whose restaurant this is."

"There'd better not be anything in my food that's not supposed to be there," Grond said. "You're a big enough player. You've got your own muscle. Why bring me in on this? And who am I fighting? The glove-tosser?"

"I've got muscle. I don't got *you*," Prescott said. "You're better than any of my guys. I'm not afraid to admit it. Any chance I could get you to quit on Rhundi and come work with me permanent?"

"Not even one," Grond said. "I owe her."

"Whatever you owed her you paid off a long time ago," Prescott said.

Grond shrugged. There were things that Prescott didn't know about, and he wasn't about to tell him any of them.

"Maybe," he said. "But I'm not leaving. What can I say; the little people entertain me."

There was a brief, poisonous moment of silence. Then Prescott laughed.

"Yeah, okay, I probably deserved that," he said. "But

yeah. I wanted you because you're better than the local talent. And I need somebody who can be prepared for anything, on short notice. I hear you're good at that."

"I'm good at that," Grond agreed. "You know the rules?"

"Dunno," he said. "Maybe to the death. Hopefully not. First blood? Surrender? Who the fuck challenges people to duels anymore anyway?"

Helpful, Grond thought. "Do you have *any* hard information? Who am I fighting?"

"I don't know that either," Prescott said. "But I've got people working on it. He isn't supposed to know who you are either."

"So this is a power play," Grond said. "You're letting him see who you've brought in in advance. That's optimistic. Anything stopping him from just having our food poisoned?"

"The challenge was pretty public," Prescott said. "Too many witnesses. I could shoot myself in the head right now in this room and he'd be blamed for it. I'm basically fuckin' immortal until the fight happens."

"May as well eat, then," Grond said, and as if by magic the food appeared. Half of it was on fire.

Probably should have actually read the menu, Grond thought.

*   *   *

Grond hadn't brought many weapons with him on his vacation— he had thought that even *he* could probably get through a chess tournament without having to kill anyone— but some things he just didn't ever leave the house without. Prescott had given him coordinates to a natural amphitheater a few dozen kilometers outside of the city limits, along with instructions to be there at noon.

Grond headed out there at midnight anyway. He brought along his favorite heavy pistol and Angela, his Iklis sniper's longbow. If the fight was going to involve shooting it was going to be very, very short; Grond could take the head off of the average gunman with Angela before they'd even managed to lay a finger on their own weapons, and the longbow nearly never missed. He'd also strapped a half-dozen knives of various lengths to his waist, forearms and calves, and just for giggles slung a war axe onto his back. He hadn't even meant to *bring* the axe; he'd found it in his luggage when he arrived. He'd forgotten to take it out of the bag the last time he'd needed it. As a last resort, he wore spiked gloves on his hands.

Showing up early had a few purposes. First, it was always good to scope out the terrain before any sort of fight. Second, he didn't trust Prescott as far as—

Well, he thought, laughing to himself. He actually had a pretty good idea of how far he could throw Prescott, having tossed Brazel on more than one occasion. Maybe he trusted Prescott *exactly* as far as he could throw him.

At any rate, if this was a setup, it was best to know in advance. Prescott probably wasn't dumb enough to try and catch Grond in a trap, but sometimes people could surprise you.

It certainly didn't look like a setup, though. The boat he'd borrowed from Rhundi to make the trip was simple enough that it didn't even have a name or a speaking AI, but she'd had a decent-quality sensor package installed for him before he left. Those sensors weren't picking up anything alive that was large enough to be sentient and nothing emitting any sort of signals for a full two kilometers around the site of the meet. Someone had carved seats out of the stone bowl of the theater at some point, but the place was old enough that they'd probably used hand tools and their own muscles to create them rather than assigning the task to bots.

He'd spend the night camped out anyway. He found a clearing far enough away from the site to not be easily located and landed his ship. The comm beeped at him. It was Rhundi.

"You're fighting a troll," she said.

Grond nearly laughed. "Do you have a nanocloud following me or something? Is there a bug in my clothes somewhere? How do you *do* that?"

"Don't worry about it," she said. "But yeah: Prescott's buddy is using a troll as his second. His name is Romnes dor Aatic din Krevaar. I've got the girls seeing what else they can find on him."

"I didn't think trolls *fought*," Grond said. He tried to remember if he'd ever fought one in the pits before and couldn't come up with one. The only troll he'd ever known well was Irtuus-bon, and Irtuus-bon was certainly no fighter.

"About that," Rhundi said. "Irtuus-bon wanted to talk to you, actually. Mind if I comm him in?"

"Sure," Grond said. There was a muted *click* and then he could hear the troll's heavy breathing at the other end of the connection.

"Grond," Irtuus-bon said. "Trolls are generally … *not* warriors."

"Tell me something I don't know, Irtuus-bon," Grond said. "I've met you. Neither you nor Sirrys could lay a finger on me if your lives depended on it." Irtuus-bon's full name was Sirrys ban Irtuus bon Alaamac. Trolls were shapechangers, and their different preferred forms generally had— or, at least, *seemed* to have— different dominant personalities and answered to different names. Sirrys was Irtuus-bon's shortest, widest form, and was childish, whiny, and petulant. The troll was far from Grond's favorite of Rhundi's employees, but he greatly preferred Irtuus-bon's company to Sirrys'.

"You have not ... met *Alaamac*, yet," Irtuus-bon said. "And you should hope that you never do." His voice deepened and roughened on the last few words, and Grond imagined the troll struggling to keep his own body together on the other end of the conversation.

"What's that mean?" he said.

"That my people are *rarely* entirely what they seem," Irtuus-bon answered. "Do *not* allow yourself to be surprised by this Romnes dor Aatic din Krevaar. I do not know of him, and I can find no information about him. This ... *disquiets* me."

"I'll be careful," Grond said. *I can't believe I'm uneasy about fighting ONE troll*, he thought.

"Please do," Irtuus-bon replied. "The mistress will not admit it, but she would be ... *highly* put out were you not to return."

Grond chuckled. "Any idea what the terms of the duel are going to be?"

"Submission," Rhundi said. "But being dead means you submitted. So don't kill him unless you have to. But *kill him if you have to*. I probably don't need to tell you that."

"Nah," Grond said. That meant that the fight was probably going to be hand-to-hand, since weapons tended to be more lethal than fists. That was fine. He hadn't come out here to die anyway. "I'll be fine, Rhundi. You know that better than anyone. I'm on stake-out for the rest of the night, so don't comm me unless it's an emergency."

"Will do," she said, and disconnected. Grond grabbed his thermal uticloak from the ship's small closet and threw it over his shoulders. It was time to find somewhere to hide out for the night.

*   *   *

The night passed uneventfully, and Grond met Prescott and another human outside the amphitheater as soon as he saw them arrive.

"What did you need me for?" he asked, eyeing the other human. He was nearly Prescott's exact opposite, standing just under two meters tall and muscular for his size.

"My partner, Stellan," Prescott said. The other man nodded. "He doesn't fight."

"He should think about starting," Grond said, shaking hands with the man. "I could probably teach him a few things."

"I'm the brains of the operation," Stellan said.

Prescott elbowed Stellan in the side. "He insisted on coming. Pay no attention to him."

Grond shrugged. "Whatever you want. I hear I'm fighting a troll."

"Rhundi?" Prescott asked.

"Yup," Grond said.

"Shit, she coulda let *me* know," Prescott said. "How the hell does Rhundi have better contacts on *my planet* than I do?"

Grond shrugged again. "You've known her about as long as I have," he said.

"Longer, I think," Prescott said. He pointed. "There," he said, and a silver dartship flew into view. "They'll be here soon. You got anything you need to do to … I dunno, get ready?"

"Nah," Grond said, rolling his neck. "Just let me know when the punching starts. I'll be ready."

"You'd better be," Prescott said.

                    *   *   *

Banik turned out to be a dapper, handsome sort of human, average height, well into adulthood, with caramel-colored skin and a teased-out shock of wiry black hair. He wore a maroon long-sleeved robe and stepped off of his ship with a snarl on his face. The troll followed. It looked much like Irtuus-bon: a sharp, hooked nose and pointed chin, a stiff shock of strawlike hair atop his head, and rolls of warty, purplish skin everywhere on his body. He was in his shortest form at the moment, assuming dwarflike proportions of just over a meter tall and nearly the same width. He looked both larger and heavier than Sirrys. He would probably be taller than Irtuus-bon in that corresponding form as well.

"This is your champion?" Banik spat. "A halfogre?"

"Grond," Grond answered. "And yeah, I'm a halfogre."

"How much did he buy you for?" the man asked.

So that's how it's gonna be, huh?

Grond allowed himself to smile. Very, very slowly, showing his teeth.

"Nah," he said. "I'm a freelancer. Means I ain't gotta follow the rules unless I decide I want to. Worst thing that happens is I lose out on a little bit of money."

He clenched a fist, loudly cracking his knuckles. Banik's eyes flickered toward his hand and his composure broke just for a moment.

"Let's get this over with," Prescott said. "You got anybody else with you?"

"Just this," Banik said, and gestured over his shoulder. A telepresence 'bot walked off the ship.

"The *Wonder of Transcendence* will be recording the proceedings," he said.

Grond, carefully arranging his weapons on the ground next to Prescott, laughed out loud. He found himself really hoping to be able to use the war axe. "That's the stupidest fucking name for a ship I've ever heard," he said.

Banik ignored the jab. "No blades or guns. The loser shall be the one who submits first, or is first unable to continue the fight."

"Got it," Grond said, and tossed a handful of dirt into the troll's eyes.

*   *   *

The first few seconds of the fight were savage, as Grond took advantage of his opponent's blindness and pounded the reeling troll in the head for all he was worth, hoping to end the duel quickly.

It didn't work. Grond had punched hundreds of skulls in his lifetime, but the rubbery way his fists contacted the troll's head were like nothing he'd ever experienced. The troll went down, but just shook its head and stood back up, wiping a quick hand across its eyes to clear the dirt out.

And it smiled at him, a tiny trickle of blood leaking from a contusion on one cheek.

"Hey," Grond said. "That's *my* move."

"This one's mine," the troll said, and punched him from two meters away, lengthening his arms in an eyeblink to hit Grond in the chin.

Right, the halfogre thought to himself. *Shapechanger.* This was going to be interesting. He was used to fighting people whose reach he could anticipate. The troll kept its distance, using its long arms, sending a flurry of punches and kicks toward Grond's head and torso, too quick for the halfogre to react to them.

Almost too quick, at least. Romnes dor Aatic din Krevaar swept a leg at Grond's ankles, trying to knock the big halfogre off his feet. Grond leapt over the swinging limb and landed heavily on the troll's ankle. With any other species, the ankle would have broken badly and the fight would effectively have been over. The troll was unable to free its foot, but the expected *snap* didn't happen. Grond improvised, grabbing Romnes' thin leg in one hand and yanking the troll toward him.

He obliged, shrinking his legs and using the momentum to ram both fists into Grond's eyes. The world flashed and Grond landed flat on his back, the troll now towering over him. Grond rolled backwards and away from his opponent, now working on keeping *his* distance.

Can't knock him out. Can't break his joints. Hmm. This was going so well.

The troll rushed him. Grond kept his center of gravity low and tried to hit him in the chest with a forearm, hoping to take the fight to the ground. Romnes dor Aatic din Krevaar shrunk his torso underneath Grond's arm and then came right back up again, hitting him in the chin with an uppercut fierce enough to rattle Grond's teeth. Grond caught the troll's extended arm by the elbow and pounded him under the ribs three times, blows that would probably have killed a human adversary. The troll shrieked in pain, the first sound he had made during the fight.

Organs. Gotcha. He wrenched Aatic-din's arm behind his back and took a few shots at his other kidney. The troll put a foot on Grond's knee and pushed away from him, wrenching his arm from Grond's grip. Grond dodged away from his counterattack and feinted another swing at his head. The troll took the bait, trying to shrink his head out of the way again, and was rewarded with an kick straight into his chin, a blow that staggered him badly, nearly costing him his footing.

A moment later, he changed shape again. This form was mid-sized, but powerfully muscled, and Grond watched as the troll's excess skin slid and hardened, forming plates of stiff armor over the vulnerable areas he had been targeting. His teeth lengthened, too, and foamy saliva began leaking from his lips.

"Oh, come on," Grond said. "Poison? Are you serious?"

"The rules were *no blades or guns*," Krevaar said. "Poison is none of those things."

"Right," Grond said. *Yeah, this is definitely going well.*

It was clear immediately that Krevaar was going to fight differently than either of the troll's other forms. The armor plating restricted his ability to lengthen and shorten his limbs, but he was hitting much harder, and now Grond needed to avoid sharp teeth as well.

And claws, he thought, as Krevaar barely missed him with an outstretched hand, tearing small furrows into his chest. The wounds burned. The troll's new claws were apparently poisonous as well.

Fuck this. The troll had changed the rules. It was time for him to do the same. He maneuvered himself in between the troll and Prescott, then leapt backwards, scooping Angela off the ground.

Banik had time to open his mouth, no doubt to complain about Grond's rule-breaking, before the halfogre fired two quick shots from the longbow.

Both struck the *Wonder of Transcendence's* telepresence 'bot, one shot taking its head off and the other reducing its torso to a smoking wreck. The troll stood up, uncertainly, its arms held out to its side.

"No guns," it said. Banik's mouth moved but no sound came out. Prescott and Stellan were quietly laughing.

Grond dropped Angela and walked to the telepresence 'bot. He grabbed one of its arms and twisted, wrenching it free of the wrecked torso.

"We're still fighting, by the way," he said, and smacked the troll across the face with the arm. The troll went down hard, and Grond hit it several more times for good measure, dropping the arm on top of his crumpled body when he was done.

He looked carefully. Hard to tell if he was breathing, since the leathery armor didn't move much.

"I think he lost," he said.

"You *cheated*," Banik said.

"Really?" Grond said, picking the arm back up.

"This ain't a blade or a gun. This is clearly an *arm*. I was using *my* arms and you weren't complaining. This is just somebody *else's*. Perfectly fair."

"I demand satisfaction—" the man sputtered. Grond hit him in the face with the arm, enjoying the visceral *crunch* as his lower jaw shattered.

"I'm pretty satisfied," he said. "Prescott? You satisfied?"

"Plenty," Prescott said. "That was worth the money he owed me."

Grond grabbed Banik by the front of his robe, lifting him off the ground, and carried him over to the troll. He wrapped a hand around the unconscious troll's ankle and dragged him along with them to Banik's ship.

"This boat looks expensive," he said to Banik, who was whimpering and trying to hold his face together. "I bet you've got access to some decent painkillers in there that will keep you from screaming too much while it flies you home. I think my friend just inherited a restaurant. Nod if you agree. Don't try to talk."

Banik nodded.

"Good," he said. "You understand I can come back if you cause any more trouble."

Banik nodded again.

"Bye now," he said, dropping him on the ground. "You can get your buddy here aboard yourself. Or just leave him here. I don't care."

He turned and walked back to Prescott and Stellan.

"Prescott says you don't fight," he said to Stellan, who nodded. "Any chance you're good at chess?"

*   *   *

THE ZIGGURAT OF ZAUMG

"That is *not* what I meant," Brazel said.

"You told Rhundi you wanted a change of pace," Grond said. "This is a change of pace. We have never, *ever* done anything like this before."

"A change of pace is like a vacation, or something *fun*," Brazel complained. "No part of that looks like any fun at all."

"I think it's pretty," Grond said.

The two of them were standing in the open cargo hold of the *Nameless*, which was hovering about fifty meters above the ground. Untamed forest spread to the horizon in every direction. Everywhere they looked was green.

Except for the giant brass ziggurat sitting in front of them. Not only was the ziggurat not green, it was *shining*. And bare. There wasn't a leaf or a weed, even a scratch, anywhere they could see.

"There are no *paths* in this forest," Brazel continued to complain. The gnome ran his hands through his arm fur, smoothing it and trying to hide the most obvious signs of his agitation. "Nothing's been near here for years. And I bet there's not so much as an *insect* on that thing. That's not natural."

He glared at Grond, his halfogre partner. It was a tricky thing to do, as they were both standing and Grond was nearly twice his height. "I am a *thief*. I am a *smuggler*. I am, on occasion, an *outside agitator*. I am not a treasure hunter."

"You didn't *have* to take the job," Grond noted. The halfogre had a broad grin on his face. He was baiting Brazel, and the gnome knew full well that this particular job was more to Grond's liking than his own. "Not everyone can raid ziggurats. Not everyone can *say* ziggurat."

"Why can't they just say *temple?* Or *pyramid?* This looks like a pyramid."

"Pyramids have sloped sides. This has levels," Grond said. "That's the difference."

"Oh, shut up," Brazel said. "How do we even get into this thing?"

"There's a shrine at the top," Grond said. "We start there. Don't even need to land."

THERE IS NOWHERE NEARBY WHERE LANDING IS POSSIBLE WITHOUT A BOMBING RUN, the *Nameless* added helpfully. I AM PERFECTLY

HAPPY TO REMAIN NEARBY TO PICK YOU UP,
HOWEVER.

"Well, so long as the *boat's* happy," Brazel said.
"What the hell do I even wear for this?" Brazel, well-
known for being meticulous about his appearance, was
sure he had nothing in his wardrobe suitable for
archaeology.

"Look on the bright side," Grond said. "Judging from
the outside, there's not gonna be a speck of dust in there.
At least your clothes won't get dirty."

The gnome made a rude gesture and headed for his
quarters. Grond sat down, his feet dangling off the edge
of the open cargo bay floor, enjoying the view.

*   *   *

The planet was called Khorbaarj. Rhundi hadn't been
sure who had named the place, and the planet wasn't
claimed by anyone. It was small, its star out-of-the-way,
and other than the trees it didn't seem to have a lot of
resources to offer. Rhundi had had an enormous smile on
her snout when she'd called them to her office, an
expression Brazel had distrusted immediately.

"How many guns should I bring?" he asked.

"Would I send my husband into danger? You know
better than that," she said.

"Sending me into danger is *half of what you do,*"
Brazel retorted. "The other half is sending *Grond* into
danger."

"That's not true at all," she answered. "You didn't fire
a single shot on your last job."

Grond made a rumbling sound deep in his chest. It
sounded like poorly-suppressed laughter.

"We were *captured.* We fought our way out with *knives and sticks,*" Brazel snapped.

"We did. It was fun," Grond said. Having spent a good part of his life as a pitfighter, he'd spent their escape reminiscing happily about old times.

"Well, you were fine," Rhundi said. "That was the point. And if you'd followed my plan, you wouldn't have been captured."

Brazel opened his mouth to argue, then closed it again.

"So, the client. Her name's Barna. She actually lives here on Arradon."

"Local?" Brazel said, an eyebrow raised. "You usually don't deal local."

"Didn't have much of a choice," Rhundi replied. "She went to Prescott first. He said he didn't have the people for the job and kicked her our way. He was rather insistent that we take it."

Brazel left this alone. Making Prescott angry could be dangerous.

"Anyway, she fancies herself an antiquities dealer. There's a structure on some little rock outside of ogrespace that she wants some people to clean out. Anything neat you find, she'll buy at a good price."

"That sounds a bit imprecise," Grond pointed out.

"Plus a convenience fee that will pay for the *Nameless'* fuel and your ammunition for three months," Rhundi replied.

"Everything is clearer suddenly," Grond said.

"What's *outside of ogrespace* mean?" Brazel asked, a suspicious look on his face.

"Just outside of ogrespace," Rhundi answered innocently.

"Okay. It's outside of ogrespace. What's it *inside?*"

"The galaxy?"

Brazel crossed his arms and flattened his ears. "It's in Benevolence space, isn't it?"

"Only a little," she said. "And there's no Benevolence presence anywhere near it. You'll be *fine.*"

"For certain values of 'fine' that include 'potentially pissing off the Benevolence,'" Brazel said. "That is not a kind of *fine* that I want anything to do with."

"Ah, c'mon, Braze," Grond said. "Treasure hunting! It sounds fun."

"I'm going to remind you of that when we're asphyxiating in the remains of our blown-up ship," Brazel said.

Grond grinned. "How? You'll be asphyxiating too."

"I'll *find a way*," the gnome said. He looked at his wife. She smiled back, not breaking his gaze.

"Screw it," he said. "I need a change of pace. She seriously gave no more specific instructions than *bring back interesting things?*"

"She literally used the word *neat*," Rhundi said. "And I did some research. If this place is important to anyone who's still around, *nobody* knows about it."

"Fine," Brazel said. "Let me pack for tomb raiding and we'll be off. I may have to buy some new clothes."

"I'll plan on leaving tomorrow," Grond said.

"Day after," Brazel said. "I don't think much will change between now and then."

*   *   *

"Just jump," Grond said. "I'll catch you. Promise."

"Right," Brazel said, and tossed a polymer ladder off the back of the *Nameless*. The peak of the ziggurat was perhaps eight meters square, with a small, cube-shaped shrine in the center. The door was sized for ogres. Brazel found himself hoping the rest of the structure was too. He wasn't looking forward to exploring the thing by himself if his partner couldn't fit through the corridors.

Grond was already testing the door by the time Brazel's feet were on solid ground. The surface of the ziggurat was surprisingly slick. He heard a slight whine in the air, some sort of resonant frequency, almost as if the entire thing was vibrating at some nearly-imperceptible level. He wondered if that was connected to the ziggurat's unnatural cleanliness.

"Any luck?"

"No hinges on the outside," Grond said. "So it either swings in or up, or maybe just slides out of the way. Haven't figured which yet. The stonework's great. I can't get a blade into the gap here." The halfogre ran his hands over the ornately carved door as Brazel walked around the shrine, inspecting it from all angles.

"There we go," Brazel heard the halfogre mumble. Anything else he may have said was drowned out by the sound of stone grinding on stone.

Grond was standing in front of the door, watching it slowly lower into the floor, a self-satisfied grin on his face.

"What did you do?" Brazel asked.

"Low-tech," the halfogre answered. "There's a catch up here in the lintel." He pointed. The catch was easily three and a half meters off the ground, and hidden on top of the protruding lintel. It would take an ogre or a troll to be able to reach the thing without climbing.

The inside of the shrine was completely dark, and smelled of stale air and age. The breeze from the doorway was surprisingly warm.

"Light up," Brazel said, activating a button on his jacket. His entire ensemble began glowing softly, providing more than enough light to see by.

"Showoff," Grond said, turning on a pair of lights mounted at his shoulders and a headlamp. "How much firepower do you have with you?"

"Very little," Brazel said. "A couple of blades. One pistol. You think we'll need it?"

"Only if we don't have it," Grond replied. "Most of what I've got with me is hand-to-hand too. I left Angela back on the *Nameless*. Didn't figure we'd have room for her." Angela was Grond's Iklis sniper's longbow. She was his most prized possession, but tight indoor spaces were not the best place for a weapon that big. He was probably carrying three times as many weapons as Brazel had anyway. Grond was not big on being caught unprepared.

The halfogre led the way, a large knife in his hand, beams of light from his lamps probing the inside of the shrine. Which proved to be entirely empty. The walls were bare stone, lacking the brass-colored covering of the outer part of the ziggurat, and bare of decoration or carving. In the center of the room was a square hole, leading further down into darkness. There was a metal ladder set into one of the sides of the hole.

"No treasure yet," Grond said.

"Great, we can go," Brazel answered.

Grond didn't bother to answer, pulling another light from a belt pouch and dropping it into the hole. It fell about ten yards, bouncing a couple of times and casting a thin light as it rolled away from the ladder.

"Bigger room down there, then. I'll go first," Grond said. Brazel watched as the halfogre started down the ladder, testing each rung first to make sure it was still able to support his weight. The gnome waited until Grond was halfway down before climbing down himself. It wasn't as annoying as he had feared. While the rungs were too widely spaced for gnomes, they were deep enough to count as ledges. The descent went easily.

"We should be in the second level," Grond said. "They'll get bigger as we go down." The room was about twice as large in either direction, with an ornate door at the center of each wall. Unlike the bare stone above, some attempt had been made to work the stone in this room, with long, sinuous shapes carved into the walls and on the floor. The stones sparkled brightly in the artificial light.

"Getting somewhere," Grond said. "You think we'll be as lucky with the doors on this one?"

"I'd try that first," Brazel said, easily scaling the lintel around the door and looking for the catch.

"Hmm," the gnome said.

"Is that a good *hmm* or a bad *hmm?*" Grond asked.

"There's a catch here, all right," Brazel said, looking closely. "But ... hell, pick me up." The halfogre reached out and set Brazel on his shoulders, and the gnome fished out a dagger and carefully prodded at something on top of the lintel.

There was a screech and a flash as two blades spun out from the corners of the lintel, coming down just in front of where Brazel's hand would have been. The door clunked, as if it had fallen a short distance.

"That would have taken your fingers off," Brazel said. "Do you remember Rhundi saying anything about traps?"

"I do not," Grond replied. "And I like my fingers." He rummaged through his pack, pulling on a pair of armored gloves. They were lightweight, but they'd turn a severed finger into a broken one, and broken ones were much easier to fix.

The two of them put their shoulders into the door, which begrudgingly slid out of the way.

The room was empty, save for debris and dust.

"This used to be wood," Brazel said. "Look around; it's clustered by the walls. Shelves, maybe, or furniture. It's just fallen apart over the years." He picked up a larger piece of trash from the floor, which crumbled to pieces in his hands.

"Look at the floor here," Grond said.

Carved into the floor was a sigil inside a circle.

"Are those snakes?" he asked.

"I think they might be," Brazel said. If they were snakes, they were an abstract representation, with hundreds of wavy shapes curled into one another. Some of them had what appeared to be sharp teeth, and forked tongues protruded from others. Brazel stared at the sigil, trying to coerce hidden meaning out of it.

For a moment, the snakes moved. Brazel jumped back, then felt silly.

"What?" Grond asked.

"Optical illusion, I think," the gnome replied. "Stare at the thing for a minute."

Grond did. "It's moving," he said. "That's impressive." He reached out a hand, brushing his fingers over the symbol, then yanked them back.

"It's *moist*," he said. "Touch it." Brazel did. The stone felt cool to the touch and had an almost rubbery texture to it.

"Weird," he said.

"Shall we keep looking?" Grond asked. "Whatever that is, I don't think we can take it with us, and we definitely can't sell it."

"Yeah," Brazel said. There were three more rooms to examine. The first two were much the same, differing only in size: a trap on the door, easily avoided, and a room with a symbol carved into the floor and the rotten remains of furniture around the outside of the room.

The final room had no catch on the door.

"I don't see a place for the blades to come out, either," Grond said. "Should we just try and push the door open and see what happens?"

Brazel dropped down off the halfogre's shoulders and looked carefully at the door. "I don't— oh. Wait a minute." His clothing began glowing more brightly.

"Take a look at this," the gnome said. "But don't get too close." Grond leaned down, peering at the part of the door Brazel was pointing at.

"That's a hole," Grond said.

"Yeah," Brazel said. "And so is this—" he pointed at another part of the door— "and this, and this, and this, and ... man, they're *everywhere.*"

"Spike trap?" Grond said.

"Probably projectiles. Any good ideas about how to trigger it?"

"I suspect opening it or pushing on it too hard will do the job," Grond said.

"So how do we get in?"

"If we're smart, we *don't*," the halfogre said. "If we're *not* smart ..." he produced a grenade from his pack.

"We blow the door altogether. Okay. Sounds fun," Brazel said. "And not at all like something that will backfire."

"Shoulda brought something shaped," Grond said. "Dumb. Ah well." The two hid behind a doorway and Grond tossed the grenade at the closed door. It exploded on impact, a cloud of dust filling the central room. They waited for a few minutes, letting the dust settle and their ears recover from the sound, then went to examine the damage.

The door was blown to pieces. Thousands of tiny needles lay scattered around the room.

"That wouldn't have been good, I'm guessing," Grond said.

"Poison, you think?" Brazel asked.

"Those wouldn't do a lot of damage to an ogre," Grond said. "And they look like they wouldn't even penetrate thick clothing. So I'm guessing poison, yeah."

"Let's see what they're protecting," Brazel said, and moved into the room, Grond following behind him.

A moment later, the floor collapsed.

*　　*　　*

"Ow," Brazel said.

He tried to move his arms and legs, which cooperated, if grudgingly. Nothing felt broken, and while he had some cuts and scrapes no part of him seemed to be in any more pain than any other part. His clothing was flickering, lending a ghostly glow to his surroundings.

Must have landed on the power supply, he thought, and looked up. The fall had to have been fifteen meters.

Lucky, he thought. *If I'd landed differently, I could be dead*.

A moment later it occurred to him to wonder what he'd landed on. The floor that had collapsed had been stone, and it had presumably landed on *more* stone. *This should hurt a LOT more than it does*.

He looked around for Grond. His partner was a couple of meters away, also beginning to stir. He didn't seem any more injured than Brazel was.

There was a hissing sound in his ears.

Wait.

Hissing?

Something crawled over his hand, and Brazel staggered to his feet.

He was standing on a large chunk what had been the floor, big enough that it looked like he had ridden it down during the fall. His lights were still struggling to reassert themselves, but he could see beyond the edges of the chunk of masonry at what he had landed on.

It was moving.

"This can't be good," he mumbled.

The floor started surging over the edges of the piece of stone he was standing on.

"Grond," Brazel said. The halfogre pushed himself up onto his elbows, shaking his head. Grond had taken a harder fall than Brazel, and had several broken pieces of stone underneath him. It looked as if whatever was moving toward Brazel was already starting to crawl over his legs.

"GROND!"

Grond shook his head again and then abruptly came to himself, swinging his arm at his legs and clearing something off himself. He stood up, unsteadily, swatting at the lights he was wearing and turning them back on.

The floor heaved.

There was almost too much going on to parse. They'd landed on a pit of living creatures at least a half-meter deep: snakes, insects, lizards, other things that didn't seem to fit into any of those categories. Some were pretty clearly mechanical. Others were feeding on each other. An alarming percentage of them were trying to reach Brazel and Grond.

"You've gotta be kidding," Grond said. Brazel found his gun and fired a few shots into the floor. His effort blew apart a few of the creeping mass but made no real difference of any kind to what was happening.

"Not kidding," Brazel said. "Any ideas?"

"Yeah," Grond said, and unhooked a device from his bandolier. "Get over here." Brazel took a couple of steps back and leaped, landing lightly on one of the pieces of floor Grond had been laying on. Grond thumbed a switch and pointed the thing he was holding at the swarming horde on the floor. There was a loud keening noise and the creatures scattered.

"Directed sonics," Grond said. "I was hoping I'd get to use this sometime." The device looked like a projectile gun with an unfolding dish in place of a barrel. Whatever sound it was making, Brazel couldn't hear it, but the scratching of millions of tiny feet and claws and the screeching sounds most of them were making now was overwhelming. Grond waved the device around, clearing the floor for a meter or so around the two of them.

"How long will that last?"

"An hour, maybe," Grond said. "And you never know, the intensity may just kill some of them. But we gotta find a way out of here." Brazel peered into the darkness around the two of them. It looked like they'd fallen into a larger room than the one above them— which made sense, since the next-lower level on the ziggurat would be bigger. But there ought to be a way out somewhere. They hadn't seen any way down from the floor above them, so it *had* to have been in here somewhere—

"There," the gnome said, pointing at the corner of the room. There was no door, but it looked like there was a passage. Grond waved the gun back and forth a few times between them and the door, and the swarm did its best to scatter.

"C'mere," he said, grabbing Brazel. "This is gonna *suck*." He deposited the gnome on his shoulders and then, stomping heavily and using the sonic gun to clear a path, worked his way toward the passageway.

"Don't trip," Brazel said.

"Ya *think?*" Grond shouted. "You get heavier when you talk." Brazel could hear the bodies crunching underneath his partner's boots, and was suddenly glad the halfogre, who tended to leave his legs bare in hotter climates, had chosen to wear pants today. There was a step up from the snake-pit into the passage, and the individuals in the swarm were too busy pulling each other down for many of them to be able to climb it. Brazel leapt as soon as they were close enough, then got out of Grond's way as he leapt the last few steps.

"Look back up there," Brazel said. Grond turned, pointing his lights back up at the floor above them. The floor had collapsed in a neat rectangular pattern.

"That was a trap, not your grenade," he said. "I like this place less with every passing minute."

"When I yell at you about this later, I'm pretending it was *your* idea, just so you know," Grond said. Brazel ignored the jab, moving along the corridor carefully, looking for anything that could be a wire or a pressure plate. The good thing about being so much smaller than his partner was that the traps would probably be sized and weighted for ogres and not for gnomes. Grond, meanwhile, was shaking things off of his boots and stomping anything left alive in the corridor.

"These were good boots, too," he said. Brazel glanced over. They were shredded. It seemed unlikely that nothing poisonous had managed to bite him, but Grond wasn't frothing at the mouth yet or anything.

The hallway looked safe. Suspiciously safe, actually.

"Give me another couple of minutes," Brazel said. "Don't go anywhere yet." Grond nodded, stomping something mechanical and many-legged into pieces and kicking its body back into the room.

A moment later, Brazel reached the end of the hall. There was no door this time, just an abrupt left turn to the hallway and then a widening stairway down into an enormous open room that had to fill the rest of the open space on that floor of the ziggurat. *Did we count the levels?* Brazel thought. There had to be at least three, but maybe this one counted as the fourth. He didn't remember how many there were from outside.

The question was knocked clean out of his head when he saw what was in the room.

Four golden, gem-studded sarcophagi were aligned in two perpendicular lines. At the intersection of the lines stood a brass-colored stand with a book sitting on top of it. The book was open. It was also *enormous*, measuring at least two meters square, and perhaps half a meter thick. The sarcophagi glittered in the light.

Wait. There was light. And it *wasn't* coming from him.

"The book's glowing," he said.

"What?" Grond said. He was still trying to clean bugs out of his boots.

"Get down here," Brazel said. "But be careful. And ... brace yourself." The halfogre loved books more than Brazel had ever loved *anything*, and it would be difficult to stop him from charging into the room and trying to read the thing. That felt like a very bad idea.

"What's that mean?" Grond asked, and then peered into the room.

"Oh," he said. "I want that."

"No," Brazel said.

"Yes," Grond said. "We told the client we'd give her *anything neat*. Nobody likes books anymore, and besides, that is not *neat*. It is *unspeakably awesome*. That means it's mine. I'll haul the coffins out for her." He leaned into the room.

"See anything on the floor to worry about?"

"No," Brazel said. "But I *really* don't trust the fact that the thing's *shining*."

"Phosphorescent ink," Grond said. "That doesn't mean *trap*."

"Central chamber of a building riddled with traps means trap," Brazel pointed out.

"So we'll be careful," the halfogre said, and headed down the stairs into the room. Brazel followed, cursing under his breath.

*   *   *

"It's called the Book of Zaumg," Grond said, carefully examining the open page. "You ever heard of Zaumg?"

"Not once," Brazel said. "You can *read* that?" The script wasn't anything he recognized. The book was open to an illustration, with little text on it other than a few lines across the top. The image was of something horrible and insectile, with dozens of legs, sharp fangs, a stinger, and a few too many wings. He found himself hoping the book was a reference text on entomology.

"You can't? Are you serious?"

Brazel looked closer. "No. I've never seen that script before."

The halfogre's eyes widened a bit. "That's just basic script, Brazel. It's in Talk. Just ordinary normal Talk."

"It's not," Brazel said. "I promise."

"That's interesting," Grond said. "Keyed to ogre genetics somehow? Is that even a thing? This looks like it's made from proper vellum. Ink looks like ink. Cover's some kind of wood. How'd they incorporate the tech to figure out who was reading it?"

"Magic, maybe?" Brazel said.

"This ain't a Benevolence tomb," Grond said. "Doesn't make sense."

"Maybe," Brazel said. "You recognize this?" He pointed at more carvings on one of the tombs.

"*That's* elf," Grond said. "I can't read elf, but I know it when I see it."

"I am suddenly liking this place less," Brazel said.

"I'm gonna open one of these," Grond said. "Then we can decide what to do with them." He looked around. All the sarcophagi had elf writing on them, but the inscriptions looked different. He and Brazel spent a few minutes carefully examining the sarcophagus for anything suspicious. Eventually the gnome stood up and shrugged.

"Stand back," Grond said, and shoved the lid. For a moment, even his strength was insufficient, and the lid didn't move. He reset his feet and pushed again, and this time the heavy gold lid was forced aside.

The sarcophagus was filled with a thick, viscous green fluid.

"Do *not* touch that," Brazel said. Grond pulled out a long, thin knife and prodded the surface. The knife hit the bottom of the sarcophagus without resistance. When Grond pulled it back out, not a drop of the fluid stuck to the blade.

Suddenly the liquid began bubbling. Simultaneously, a loud grinding sound shattered the silence in the room. The doorway was beginning to close, a huge stone block dropping from the ceiling. Grond turned and sprinted to the door, but wasn't close to being in time.

The light from the book winked out, leaving them alone in the dark.

"Can you smell— oh, *hell*," Brazel said. The bubbly liquid was turning gaseous, the mist rolling out of the sarcophagus and pooling on the ground.

"Time to go," Grond said.

"The way out just *closed,*" Brazel said. "You have another grenade?"

"Don't need one," Grond said. "We need a way *out*. And we have a spaceship. Namey, you out there?" The two retreated to the top of the stairs. The gas from the sarcophagus had already filled most of the floor of the room, and was beginning to rise.

ARE YOU READY TO BE PICKED UP? the *Nameless* answered via comm. I DO NOT SEE YOU YET.

"Yes and no," Grond said. "We kinda need you to blow a hole in the bottom level of this thing. Like, *now.*"

A CARDINAL DIRECTION WOULD BE USEFUL, Namey replied. WHICH PART DO YOU WISH ME TO BLOW UP?

"Triangulate us and *blow up the other side,*" Brazel shrieked. "I didn't bring a compass!"

FINE, the boat said. I SUGGEST YOU GET UNDERNEATH SOMETHING.

A moment later, there was an enormous explosion and the room suddenly flooded with light.

"Go!" Grond shouted. "I'll be right behind you!"

Brazel fled, then realized why the halfogre was *behind* him.

"LEAVE THE DAMN BOOK, GROND!"

His partner had the book off of the podium and closed, and was staggering under the weight. Meanwhile, the gas from the sarcophagus appeared to be *acidic*. He heard a frightening hissing sound that seemed to be coming from his pants. He had a moment to think *I've never worried about my pants dissolving off before* and then the *Nameless* flew into view, the open cargo bay door visible through the dust from the explosion. He leapt, scrabbling onto the ship.

He heard "MOVE!" from behind him, and barely managed to scramble out of the way before the book hit the floor of the bay, landing alarmingly close to where his head had been. A moment later, Grond pulled himself aboard, quickly rolling onto his back and kicking his ruined boots and steaming leggings off his body and off the boat.

"Ow," he said. HIs legs and feet would be acquiring a few more scars.

"You saved the book. You *nearly died* to save the *book*," Brazel said. "You understand that means we're selling it. We didn't grab anything else."

"I grabbed a handful of jewels off one of the sarcophagi," Grond said. "That's gotta count for something."

"We'll argue about it later," Brazel said. "Stow that thing and then get yourself into the medbay. I don't need your legs rotting off. And we're charging whatshername for my pants."

Grond checked the book for damage, then ran his hand over the cover, admiring the detail in the woodcutting. He'd have time to read it when they were home, after he'd won the inevitable arguments with Brazel and Rhundi over getting to keep the thing. Hopefully the jewels would be enough to mollify their client. They hadn't *guaranteed* anything, after all.

Below them, in a room now dense with green mist, the lids of three golden sarcophagi slid open and clattered to the floor.

*　　*　　*

DEBUT

"Are you sure about this?" the halfogre said.

"As sure as I'll ever be," the gnome responded. "She'll be fine. It's a milk run."

"Every time anybody says *milk run* around here somebody ends up getting shot, Rhundi."

"Which is why I keep saying it," she said. "Gotta keep you boys on your toes, and all."

"We telling Brazel?"

Rhundi chuckled. Letting her husband know that their daughter Darsi was getting sent on a run was probably the right thing to do, but she was pretty sure that Brazel would spend every moment between finding out and her departure filling her head with advice and suggestions. Rhundi needed the kid's head clear, and she had a job or two for Brazel along the way anyway.

"We are not," she said. "Not until after she's gone."

The big halfogre leaned back in his chair in her office, smiling and knitting his hands behind his bald, scarred head. He was twice her size, and the chair was the largest piece of furniture in the room. It made for an interesting sight. "You got something for us to fill our time with, then?"

"Something for *him* to do," she said. "I'm not sending you along with either of them, and I think it's best if I don't know where you are for the next few days. There's gotta be a chess tournament around for you to get involved in, right, Grond?"

Grond nodded, reading between the lines easily enough. "I'm sure I can find something if I look hard enough," he said.

*   *   *

Darsi Tavh're'muil was on her way back to her quarters after school when the comm message came through from her mother.

"My office," Rhundi said. "Right now. Unless you have something more important to do."

"You know I don't," Darsi said. Rhundi owned a decent-sized chunk of the *planet* they lived on, and the intergalactic resort they all lived in was the center of her empire. There was no point in even pretending that Rhundi wasn't fully aware of where she was or what she was doing at any given time; she probably had nanocameras sewn into her *clothes*.

Not that she minded overly much. Being the boss's oldest daughter had its advantages, and one of those advantages was an overly protective 2.4-meter tall halfogre. It was worth the trade for a little parental surveillance. She sent a quick comm to her next-youngest sister letting her know she'd be late getting home and headed toward her mother's office. She was there in a few minutes. Gorrim, her mother's secretary, waved her past when he saw her.

"She's waiting for you," he said.

"Any idea what this is about? Is Dad in there?"

"He came in the back way, if he is," Gorrim answered. He had an amazingly deep voice for a gnome. She'd known him for years, and it still took her by surprise every time he opened his mouth. "Grond came out a few minutes ago. Said he was taking a couple of days off and not to go looking for him. Didn't look too happy."

That's weird, she thought. Darsi's mother had known Grond since before Darsi was born— she'd met the halfogre before she'd met her *father,* even— and in all that time she'd never known the two to argue. Grond was fiercely protective of Rhundi even considering that he was technically one of her bodyguards, and he'd transferred that allegiance to her husband and each of their many children as they'd come along. She hoped nothing was wrong.

The door slid open, and Darsi went into the office.

Her mother sat behind her desk, which for the moment looked like a giant slab of reflective stone. Rhundi's desk had a holoprojector built into it and she was fond of altering its appearance, sometimes going through several styles over the course of a single week. Atop the desk sat a silver box, a cube perhaps forty centimeters on each side.

"Hi, Mom," Darsi said. "I like your fur." Rhundi's

fur was normally a golden-brown color, slightly darker than Darsi's, but she rarely went with her natural shade. The last time Darsi had seen her she'd had the tips of her fur tinted green; the green was gone now, replaced with handprint-sized blue rosettes scattered everywhere. One of them surrounded one of her eyes. The effect made her look less like the mostly-legitimate businessperson she thought of herself as and more the smuggler she'd been before Darsi was born.

"Thanks," Rhundi said, pointedly *not* mentioning her daughter's look, which involved shaved patches. Darsi noticed the omission and didn't bother mentioning it, as irritating her parents was half the reason for the hairstyle.

"Is everything okay?" Darsi asked. "Gorrim said Grond left here earlier looking angry."

"Okay enough," Rhundi said. "Don't worry about Grond. He's taking a couple of days off. We need to talk about *you*."

Darsi looked around. "Unless Dad's hiding in a corner somewhere, you don't want him here for this talk." She brightened. "Are you sending me on a job?"

Good girl, Rhundi thought. "If you think you can handle one," she said.

"I could have *handled* one two years ago," Darsi said. "But you wouldn't let me go anywhere without an escort."

"Well, you're old enough now," Rhundi answered. "I'm issuing you a one-person skiff. This is a delivery job. You take this box, meet with your contact, hand it over, accept payment, and come back. Simple."

"What's in the box?" Darsi asked.

"A datapad that scrolls the sentence *you have failed at your mission* across the screen," Rhundi said. "None of your business, and I'm not giving you the code to unlock the case, either."

"So it's a milk run," Darsi said. "You could give this job to a 'bot if you wanted to."

"I'm giving it to *you*, which had better be good enough," Rhundi said tersely. Her eyes had suddenly turned steely. "*If* you intend to be a part of this organization, young lady, you'll learn *first* that you take the jobs I give you."

Darsi lowered her eyes. "Yes ma'am. I'll get it done."

"Good," Rhundi said, her tone returning to normal. "One more thing. I want you to take this with you."

She laid a pistol on top of the box. Darsi's eyes widened slightly and she picked up the gun. It was an expensive little number; dual-chambered for energy or projectiles, but somehow small enough that even a gnome barely into adulthood would have little difficulty concealing it.

"This isn't the one you gave me last time," she said. It hadn't been *that* long since they'd last had to flee the resort, and Rhundi had left Darsi in charge of all of her siblings. She'd sent her armed.

"No," Rhundi said. "That was more of a last resort. You're not going to have one of my security teams as backup this time. You need something with a bit more stopping power."

Darsi nodded, then leaned forward and put the gun back on the box.

"I don't want it," she said.

"Interesting," Rhundi said. "Explain."

"I'm not a good shot," she said. "You know that. If you thought there was a chance I'd need to fire that thing, I wouldn't be going, or at the *very least* you'd have me seconded to Dad or Grond or both of them. Which means you're offering it to me to see if I'm scared enough to take it."

She looked her mother directly in the eye.

"And I'm not," she said. "I can take care of myself."

"And if something goes wrong?" Rhundi said. "I'm not sending backup with you. You know that."

"I get out of it without killing anyone," she said. "I didn't say I was going to go completely unarmed. I'm just not taking a gun. If I take a gun, it's going to find an excuse to get used."

Rhundi nodded.

"Talk to Tarrysh about your boat," she said. Tarrysh was the resort's head of security. "You leave tomorrow."

"Is there a dossier?" Darsi asked. "I'd like to know where I'm going before I leave."

"In your quarters already," Rhundi said. "Any other questions?"

"You're really not going to tell Dad?"

"I'm leaving that up to you," she said. "You know how he'll react. If you want a constant stream of advice between now and you leaving, let him know."

"Grond already knows, doesn't he." It wasn't a question.

"Yes," Rhundi confirmed. "He wanted to go with you. I told him to take a couple of days off."

Darsi nodded. "All right," she said. "I'll be ready."

"You already are," Rhundi responded. Darsi nodded, and turned to leave the office.

"You gonna take this with you?" Rhundi asked, pointing at the box.

"I wasn't, actually," Darsi said. "If that's sensitive enough that you don't want me poking around in it, I figure it's safer in here than around my brothers and sisters."

"Right answer," Rhundi said. "Go on. I'll see you for dinner in a few hours."

*   *   *

Darsi considered comming her father, and then decided that finding him in person sounded like a better idea. She was pretty sure that she knew where to find him anyway: he'd recently acquired a new ship, and so he was probably in their private hangar tinkering with it. There was, despite her mother's concerns, no chance that she was leaving the planet without talking to Brazel first.

She was right; she could hear swearing before she even got into the hangar. *Good*, she thought. It meant he was enjoying himself. Her father got deadly quiet when he was genuinely upset about something. Loud swearing meant he was relaxing.

She still hadn't gotten used to the new *Nameless*. The boat was an odd combination of cargo ship and warship, or perhaps a warship that wanted to be *mistaken* for a cargo ship at a safe distance: the cockpit was in the front, sweeping back to a wide rectangular storage bay, with all the engines together in one mass in the back. And it *bristled* with weaponry; she'd heard that her father and Grond had actually managed to *shoot down* a few Benevolence spiderships in their last engagement, which was amazing. Every previous time they'd encountered the Benevolence in deep space, the goal had been to escape them as quickly as possible. The previous *Nameless* had been caught by several spiderships at once and had been blown to pieces practically without even fighting back.

It also featured active camouflage, meaning that the color could be altered by the pilot however she or he wanted. It had been a riot of red and gold when Brazel had acquired it; he'd toned it down to a deep golden-brown. She wondered if he'd matched his own fur deliberately or if that had been an accident. The ship certainly looked nice in the new color.

Brazel was at the top of a set of wheeled stairs, energetically doing ... *something* on one of the ship's side panels. Darsi watched him for a moment, then grabbed a toolbox full of power tools and climbed up the stairs to him.

"Anything I can help with?" she asked.

Brazel turned toward her, and Darsi immediately understood the reason for the swearing. He had been cleaning *something* off of the side of the ship and whatever fluid he'd been using had managed to get all over him, ruining a pair of what he probably thought of as his good work coveralls. Her father was one of the toughest people she knew, exceeded probably only by her mother, but his one weakness was a love of expensive, stylish clothing. Grond would go to repair the ship wearing whatever he happened to have on and barely notice what happened to it; her father was the type of gnome to have *more than one* pair of "good coveralls."

She snickered. Her father glared at her.

"I'm actually almost done," he said. "Just had a little mishap. Had to get the shit off the ship before it started setting on the armor."

"I'm surprised you didn't clean yourself off first," she said.

Brazel shrugged. "Gives me an excuse to buy another

pair," he said. "And an excuse to visit the baths. What's up?"

"There's a dossier waiting for me at home. Mom gave me a job."

Brazel raised an eyebrow. "I didn't know about that. Which I assume was intentional."

"She said it was up to me whether to tell you or not. She was worried about unwanted advice."

Brazel laughed. "No. Well, okay, yes— I've been thinking about it and I have a list somewhere of about fifty things you need to consider before you head out."

"Thinking about it?" she said. "What, did Grond tell you?"

"No," Brazel said. "I've been thinking about it since you were a little girl. It was obvious *really* quick that you were going to take after your parents."

"So, no advice?" she said.

"C'mere," Brazel said, heading back down the stairs. Darsi followed him down the stairs and into his quarters on the ship.

"I have two things for you," he said. "The first is this." He handed her a thin, leather-bound notebook, tied closed with a ribbon.

"Actual leather and paper?" she said. "Not a datapad?"

"Written in my own handwriting, even," he said. "That's the fifty things. I guess Grond's rubbed off on me over the years." The halfogre loved books.

"Here's the most important thing in there," he said. "Just in case you don't read it. *Do your own research.*"

"I've heard you say that before," she said.

"Because it's important," he said. "Do your own research even if it's your own mother, who loves you deeply, sending you off on the job. Because even she misses stuff sometimes, and it wouldn't surprise me *at all* to discover that she left some details out to see how you react."

Darsi nodded.

"Here's the second thing," he said, handing her a pistol. "It's—"

"Mom already tried to give me a gun," she interrupted. "I'm not taking a gun."

"That strikes me as poor decision-making," Brazel responded. "Guns are useful. Guns that are small enough that they don't get noticed and taken away from you are even better."

"No," she said. "Not for a delivery mission. No guns."

Brazel shrugged. "Your choice," he said. "Just be open to changing your mind if you discover you need to."

"I will," she said. "I took one when I needed to defend my brothers and sisters. But not for this."

"So be it," Brazel said, hugging his daughter. "Any point to saying *comm me if you need anything?*"

"Already knew it," Darsi said, hugging him back.

*   *   *

Hours later, Darsi sat on her bed in her room, going through the dossier her mother had left for her and pondering the idea of leaving before the morning. The planet she was being sent to was called Untkaar. She'd never heard of it before, but the dossier explained that it was an unclaimed planet in the large demilitarized zone between ogre and Benevolence space. Being closer to the Benevolence than she needed to be gave her the shivers, but she put that thought away. This was going to be the first time, but it certainly wasn't going to be the last. The planet itself was a basic diverse terrestrial, with no one biome dominating any other, and two uninhabitable moons. The contact she was to meet was named Fahrhad. There was no description provided of Fahrhad at all; not even a race. *Odd,* she thought. The name sounded like it was probably a male, and probably a human, gnome, or ogre, at that; the odds of meeting with a dwarven male were pretty low and the name didn't fit the dwarven style anyway, and most elven given names were nouns or adjectives.

He could be something else, she thought. But even the less populous races rarely used single names. No troll would go by one, and no goblin had a given name. She didn't know as much about the fae or the korrylen, but she didn't think it too likely that Fahrhad was one of them either.

She kept reading, and eventually discovered a passphrase that Fahrhad was to use to identify himself, or herself, or xirself, depending on what Fahrhad actually was. There was one for her too. Well, that would make things easier.

The drop was scheduled five days away. The trip would take three through tunnelspace, meaning that she'd have some time to land and scope out the neighborhood thoroughly before she was due to meet Fahrhad. That seemed manageable.

She thought about it and threw the dossier into a bag, deciding to leave right away anyway. There was no reason to wait until tomorrow other than that her mother had planned for her to, and her voiceprint would get her into the office to collect the box. More time to spend on

Untkaar meant that she'd be better prepared for the handoff to go successfully.

If there was one thing she'd learned from her father, it was that there was never any way to be too prepared.

*   *   *

Tarrysh wasn't at the hangar any longer, but she'd left instructions releasing a boat called the *Debut* into Darsi's care. Darsi smiled at the ship's identicode, wondering if they'd changed the ship's name just for her. It was, as her mother had said, a one-person skiff, although the "one-person" measurement was scaled to bigs, meaning that she'd have plenty of room to spread out in the thing. She adjusted her bag on her shoulder and rattled the package, wondering again what was inside it.

She liked the ship. It looked fast, for one thing. The engines were oversized for the body of the ship, and there were nodules on the underside and top of the ship that hinted at hidden weaponry, although if she got into a scrap it would probably better to be fast and maneuverable and heavily shielded. The ship was probably a bit overshielded as well, but she wouldn't know that until she was inside—

—the port-side door was open, and there was a light on inside.

There was someone in her ship.

For a brief fraction of a second she regretted not letting her parents give her a gun, then she remembered where she was. There was *no way* anyone was sabotaging her ship on Arradon before she'd even left. That might be something to worry about on Untkaar, but not yet. Surely not yet.

"Who's there?" she called out.

A large shadow detached itself from the inside of the ship.

Oh.

"Hi, Grond," she said, as the huge halfogre unfolded himself through the doorway.

"Thought you weren't leaving yet," he replied. "I left something in there for you."

"Decided to take off a bit early," she said. "No reason not to."

Grond grinned. "And you weren't even gonna say goodbye, huh?"

"Mom said you split already," she said. "You done bugging my ship? How long is it going to take me to find all of them?"

Grond looked offended. "Not a one," he said. "I really did leave a present for you in there."

"I'm going to look anyway," she said.

"Good girl," he answered.

"You want to come see me open it, or are you taking off?" she asked. "It'd better not be a gun. Mom and Dad *both* tried to give me a gun already."

"It's not a gun," he said. "Promise. Something a little bit more your style."

"Speaking of *style*," she said. "I actually could use your help for something, if you have a few minutes."

"All right," Grond said. "What did you have in mind?"

"Come aboard," she said.

*   *   *

The present, as it turned out, really was a great idea— a custom electroshock staff, dual-tipped, and fitted to her build. The thing was dented and scuffed up to look like a discarded piece of junk, but Darsi knew good work when she saw it, and she could tell that Grond had started with something expensive and then torn it apart and rebuilt it to her own specifications and his own standards, including making it look like something no one would want to steal. Darsi had been training in stickfighting since she was little, mostly with Grond as her trainer. She loved the thing instantly.

"It'll need a name," Grond said. "But not yet. Give it some time, use her a few times, *then* name her." His own prized weapon was an Iklis sniper's longbow named Angela. She'd never asked him where the name had come from.

"So what did you need?" he asked.

"What do you see when you look at me?" she asked.

"My boss's kid," he said.

She snorted. "That doesn't help. What does *anybody else* see when they look at me?"

"A baby," Grond said. "I'm guessing you don't want me pulling punches here."

"No," she said. "You're right. I'm young, and I'm a *gnome*, and anybody who isn't a gnome is going to immediately assume I'm a weakling. And my style is a little too … I don't know…"

"You look like your parents own things," Grond volunteered.

"Close enough," she said. "So I need you for something." She fished around in her bag and pulled two objects out.

Grond's eyes widened. "Your mother will *kill me in*

my sleep," he said.

"Which is why you're going to help me, because if you make me do it myself, I'll make sure she knows that, and then she'll have a *reason to,*" Darsi said.

The halfogre grinned. "Yeah, she will," he said. "Okay, fine. What did you have in mind?"

*   *   *

Darsi ran her hands over her bare arms, shivering at the unfamiliar touch and wincing a bit at the pain. She'd shaved small patches of her fur off in the past, but removing all the fur from both arms was a genuinely radical move for any gnome, and she'd never even *met* one who had dared to shave off any facial fur before. She was pleased at how muscled her blue-skinned arms had turned out to be under all the fur, and the full-sleeve tattoo Grond had applied to her left arm looked *fantastic*. Her fur grew back quickly, so it would take no more than a week for that tattoo and the second one around her right eye and ear to become completely invisible. Best of all, Grond was both fast with the tattoo gun and impressively talented. The halfogre had acquired his tattoos from a variety of sources at a variety of times during his life and his tattoos were, charitably, rather *eclectic*, but the designs he'd created for her made her look a decade older and *just* dangerous enough that she wouldn't be immediately disregarded. And he'd managed the job in an hour, so she hadn't even really lost any time.

"Keep everything clean until you get to Untkaar," Grond said. "Wash it twice as often as you think you need to. You'll be healed up in a day or two but I suspect once you get where you're going you'll want to be not too pretty for a little while. We'd both prefer to not need to explain a system-wide infection to your mom when you get back."

She promised that she would, and meant it. Grond had tousled what remained of the fur on her head and left the ship without another word.

It was time to go.

*   *   *

The trip to Untkaar was uneventful. In fact, it was boring. There had been a suggested set of tunnelspace coordinates in the dossier, and all she'd had to do was enter them into the *Debut's* computer and spend the rest of the trip training and studying. The staff really was perfectly fitted for her, and she spent a few hours a day working up a sweat and going through the forms Grond had taught her.

The planet, from orbit, was actually pretty beautiful. About a third of it was water, with the remaining parts divided among mountainous or desert areas and *purple* vegetation. It was surprising that the place hadn't been claimed by anyone yet; if nothing else, the unique vegetation might make it a decent tourist destination.

Oh well. Maybe the entire place smelled of eggs or something. She'd figure it out when she landed. She went over the dossier one more time, orbiting just outside of the path the larger of the two moons took, and then had the *Debut* do a scan to see if there was any sort of authority she needed to register her ship with before she landed. It didn't look like there was, and politically the planet was mostly either unincorporated or de facto city-states around the larger population centers.

"In we go, then," she mumbled to herself, and requested a descent toward the closest city to the handoff. Unfortunately, it looked like she wasn't going to get to see any of the purple forests up close unless she decided to go sightseeing; she was headed to what probably either was or had started off as a mining center, located in a little pocket of flat land at a bend in one of the mountain ranges. The place was called Rainwyr; it had mountains on three sides and seaside on the third, so hopefully it would be scenic.

As she got closer, she revised that expectation. Rainwyr was clearly a *current* mining town, or at least there was a *lot* of mining going on near it, as there was smoke rising from half a dozen different spots in the mountains near the city. The ocean took on a distinctly greenish hue near Rainwyr that melted into more normal-looking blue the farther away it got, too. Whatever was going on there, they either lacked the technology or the priorities to avoid polluting their environment.

The comm system got a ping directing her to a berth in a spaceport on the north part of town; this worked out nicely, since that was the same side of town as the meeting. Ground control didn't ask a single question; the entire process seemed to be automated. There wasn't even any communication about berthing fees. *Somebody's going to try and shake me down*, she thought. Great; she may as well establish herself quickly as someone not to be trifled with once she landed.

The port wasn't especially busy; it looked like only about half of the available space was filled, and Darsi selected an isolated berth for the *Debut* to set down in. More foot traffic nearby might lead to some safety in numbers, but she felt like prioritizing anonymity was a better idea. She stowed away the case in a hidden storage area in her quarters and hung her staff over her back to go explore. She wouldn't go to the meeting place today, but learning the lay of the land— and possibly finding something to eat that wasn't the nonperishable stuff she'd brought with her— was still a good idea. She dressed in simple traveler's clothes, leaving her arms uncovered. She checked a mirror and decided that she looked tough enough to not scan as an easy mark but not so tough that anyone would assume she was out for trouble.

She set her face carefully before leaving the ship. It was the first time she'd been off-planet by herself, and it wouldn't do to look too much the tourist. She also half-expected a welcoming committee to be outside, and braced herself for trouble.

She was wrong; the berth was empty, with only a blinking console set next to the way out. The console specified a reasonable-sounding rate to keep the ship; she paid for a couple of days more than she thought she needed and set a passcode to keep the gate locked. Rhundi had provided her with a fairly comfortable expense account to draw on, so she had no real reason to be stingy.

*   *   *

Rainwyr was … boring. There was a strip of buildings on the edge of town, nearest the mines, that almost qualified as "bustling," but the first general store she poked her head into had prices in *scrip* and not in actual money, and the human behind the counter looked at Darsi strangely when she suggested she might buy something. Chances were the workers, whatever and whoever they were, were locked to the mines for most of their waking hours. The whole stretch probably got real busy right around payday, then settled back down again after sucking up all the money the miners had managed to eke out. There was a residential area that only escaped slum status by virtue of being relatively new, but would surely be so within a decade or so. A wide thoroughfare and a high fence surrounded what was probably a wealthier district where the managers and bosses lived. She didn't see many actual people, but most of what she saw were human, with the occasional gnome or ogre to liven up the mix. Most of them were dressed the same, in earth-toned work clothes that were probably company-issue. No dwarves, no elves, which wasn't too surprising. No one paid any attention to her whatsoever.

The place *stank*, too, badly enough that she was surprised any gnomes managed to live in Rainwyr at all. Gnomes were generally proud of their acute sense of smell, but there were times when it was less helpful than others, and this was one of them. Her theory about the rotten eggs was wrong, but the air had a sharply acidic stink to it, with a tinge of rot underneath. The smell was worse toward the ocean, although Darsi didn't see the source of the pollution anywhere. Underground pipes, probably, carrying some sort of slurry or runoff from whatever they were mining up there. That was probably the source of the rot. If there was anything in the water nearby, it wasn't surviving what the miners were doing to it.

I probably ought to find out what it is, she thought. She heard her father in her head. *Always do your own research*. And she hadn't bothered to find out what the main export of this place was, or what was getting dumped into the water not too far from where she'd landed her ship. *Sloppy*. Well, she had time to find out before the drop.

I don't like this place very much, she thought, changing her mind about finding the meetup right away. The coordinates were just north of town. It looked like she had enough time to at least give the general area a once-over before darkness hit. She'd spend the night on the ship. Maybe tomorrow she'd manage to find some fresh food. The place was right next to an ocean. On most planets, that meant an abundance of fresh food. Rainwyr appeared to be the exception, but maybe there were businesses nearer the shore that didn't take scrip.

She almost commed her father on the spot when she figured out where the coordinates were. It was an ogre bar. Her mother had sent her to make a drop at a goddamned *ogre bar*. Grond had once failed to tell Brazel that a job was happening in an ogre bar, and her father had had to crawl out of a window in the kitchen after a scrap went south. Brazel claimed it was the last time he'd broken his research rule. Grond had actually *thrown him* at their target during the fight.

There was no way this was an accident.

The good news was it was a good enough distance out of town, far enough that she was able to find a place to inconspicuously keep an eye on the door for nearly an hour. She took a deep breath. Other than the expected scents that she associated with ogres and their cooking, there were several different kinds of alcohol, most of them cheap-smelling, with a stale undertone she didn't quite recognize. She only saw a few ogres go in and out, all of them male.

It took a while for it to sink in. The place was

probably a brothel. *Please don't let the place be a brothel.* There wasn't a name on the outside or anything. If she could find out what it was *called* that would probably let her know the nature of the place. The idea of ogres passing up the chance for a crude joke as the name of a whorehouse outside of a mining town ...

It's called the Deep Shaft. I bet everything I will ever own that the name of this filthy place is the Deep Shaft.

Half of her wanted to collapse into giggles and the other half was disgusted beyond her ability to even think about it.

And I have to go in there the day after tomorrow.

Hopefully the time of the drop wasn't during Happy Hour. She'd worry about that later. It was time to get back to the ship.

                    *   *   *

Other than 'always do your own research,' the thing that Darsi's father had done his best to drive into her head was that she should always trust her own instincts. So when the fur on the back of her neck raised for no good reason as she approached the berth the *Debut* was occupying, she listened and slowed down. She pulled the staff off her back, quickly testing the resistance on the activation studs for the electroshocks at either end. The spaceport was abandoned other than her.

As far as she could see, anyway. It was getting awfully dark. *Infrared goggles.* She needed a pair of infrared goggles, and she should have grabbed a pair before she left. She flattened herself against the wall, moving quietly toward the gate.

There was a cheap hackbox attached to the entry

console. The gate was open, if only by a hair.

They wouldn't have left it behind. Cheap or not, it wasn't like the things were single-use. There was definitely still someone in there. Quite possibly more than one someone. With her ship.

The only thing to do now was to decide what to do about that.

*   *   *

"Okay." she said to herself. *"I can do this."*

What would her parents do? What would Grond do?

They would go in and scare the hell out of whoever was screwing with her ship, that's what they'd do. She didn't have that option. She wasn't *scary*.

Do your own research. Knowledge first. Figure out who was in there. She looked around. Going in through the gate was a bad idea. But the walls around the berth weren't that high. She could climb. She tossed the staff onto her back again and found a spot where she could scramble up to the top of the wall.

All right. The wall was a meter thick and three high. Plenty of room for her to hide or move around if she needed to.

There were three of them. She got into position just in time to see one of them break into the *Debut*.

Shit. The locks on the boat weren't terribly complicated. This wasn't supposed to be a dangerous enough job that she needed high-level security.

The two that stayed outside were human, one male, one female. The third *probably* was human but he ducked inside the ship too quickly for her to be sure. One was holding a long rifle. The other had some sort of pistol. She was too far away to see if it was a projectile or energy gun.

Binoculars. Binoculars and infrared. Hell, any pair of quality infrared goggles would have the binocs built in. *Stupid.*

She had three choices. The first was to let them do whatever they were doing. That was unacceptable. The second was to stop them. That was *probably* the best option but three on one wasn't odds that she liked. The third was to let them do whatever they were doing and then follow them afterward and see if something would happen to let her even those odds a bit.

The sound of a pistol being cocked at her ear reminded her of a possible fourth option.

This isn't going well.

*   *   *

"Stand up," a voice said. Human. Male. "Do it slowly. And keep your hands up."

"How do I stand up without using my hands?" she asked.

A moment of confused silence. "Just … just *do* it, okay?" the voice said.

Young. Possibly younger than her, developmentally, and inexperienced to boot. And standing in *exactly* the wrong place.

She pulled her knees tight to her chest, which lifted the end of her staff off the ground. The business end of the staff made heavy contact with whoever was behind her. She hadn't *quite* hit him exactly where she'd wanted to, but he staggered and fell backwards off the wall anyway.

But not without crying out in pain first.

She watched as the two guards outside the *Debut* snapped to attention, looking straight toward her, weapons up. The one with the rifle fired a couple of exploratory shots in her direction while the other moved back toward the ship, saying something to the person inside. Darsi dropped flat, risking a look back at where the one who had gotten the drop on her had fallen. He was up, but running away already, limping heavily. She was glad she hadn't hurt him too badly.

Firing back would probably be a good idea, she thought, suddenly regretting not having brought a gun. She couldn't see the one the runner had had. It had either gone flying when he landed or he'd taken it with him. She scrambled toward the gate as the other three thieves fled. It didn't *look* like any of them had the box. It was a little too big to conceal easily for anyone smaller than an ogre, and they still all looked human.

I need to keep one of them, she thought. She needed to know who these people were, and if they were breaking into her ship just because that's what people *did* around here or if it was connected to the job she was supposed to do. Luckily for her, one of them was a step slower than the other two. She waited for them to pass through the gate, all three of them turning in the same direction to run away, and she dropped off the wall onto the last one's back.

That was the plan, anyway. The last one out was the female, and she stumbled on something as she was turning. What Darsi intended to be a graceful leap onto her back turned into both of her feet slamming into the human's shoulders and taking her straight to the ground.

Darsi heard and *felt* it as the girl's neck and shoulders

broke underneath her.

Oh, no. She hadn't intended to kill her, and the thieves hadn't really tried to take her out, either. She'd just seriously raised the stakes, and for no good reason.

The second one stopped running, hearing the commotion behind her. The one who had broken into the *Debut* didn't, disappearing off into the distance.

He was the one with the rifle. Darsi snatched the girl's pistol off of her hip, pointing it at him and silently hoping the thing wasn't bio-locked.

"You killed her," he said. "Why did you kill her?"

Tears streaming down his face. This was his sister, or his mate, or *something*. He'd forgotten about the rifle, which fell out of his hands as he dropped to his knees.

"Why did you kill her?" he asked again. "Nothing bad was supposed to happen. This was supposed to be *easy*."

"You need to come with me," she said, keeping him covered with the gun. "Right now."

*   *   *

It only took a few minutes to get the girl's body— and *girl* was the right word, as neither her nor the other thief were grown adults yet— out of sight and the rifleman handcuffed on the *Debut*. He'd gone compliant, doing everything she asked without complaining. He was obviously in shock. Whoever these kids were, they made her look like a hardened mercenary.

They weren't siblings, or at least they *probably* weren't. He was dark-skinned, tall and thin, as if he hadn't finished growing into his body yet. She was petite and much lighter skinned. They appeared to be about the same age, maybe sixteen or seventeen standard years old.

The inside of the *Debut* had been tossed pretty thoroughly, but the third thief hadn't managed to find the box. He'd left another one behind, though, this one wooden. It smelled of blood. She *really* didn't want to know what was in it.

Darsi's head was swimming. She'd known for years that her parents— and Grond, who might as well be a surrogate parent— were killers. She didn't really want many of the details. But she wasn't ready to become one. Not by *accident*. The first time she killed someone was supposed to be for a good reason.

She shook her head. *This isn't the time.* Just because she'd never killed anyone before was no reason to fall apart in front of this kid— who, she reminded herself, had shot at her *first*.

She took a deep breath, calming herself and clearing her doubts from her head.

"Explain," was all she said. She'd secured the gun, but kept her staff to hand and between the two of them. This guy wasn't about to break the cuffs she had him in.

"It was two days' wages for just *watching*," he said. "And in *money*, not scrip. We ... we're both laid off from the mines right now. No money coming in. Xe said to watch for anybody paying too much attention to the ship and to scare them off. I've never even fired a gun before."

"Xe?" *An elf.* Interesting.

"Yeah," he said. "Paid us in advance and everything. It wasn't ... this wasn't supposed to happen."

"Who is the girl to you?"

"A friend," he said. "I've known her for a long time."

"She have a name?"

"Lee," he said. "I'm Anzel." He looked at her
expectantly.

"So the elf either didn't know my name or didn't
bother sharing, huh?" she asked. "Xe tell you xir name?"

"Xe said it was Relict," Anzel said. "I don't know if I
believe xir or not."

"What's xe look like?"

Anzel shrugged. "Like an elf. They all kinda look
the same to me, honestly. Scars all over xir face, but
other than that I couldn't tell you anything. Xe kinda kept
covered up."

Scars? Every elf she'd ever met, which wasn't many,
had made regular use of skin rejuvenation. "Old?
Young?"

"Who knows?" he said. "I don't even know how old
you are."

Provincial, she thought. The kid had grown up here,
and this Relict was probably the first elf he'd ever laid
eyes on. It was a wonder he was getting the pronouns
right. Lots of times humans didn't bother and just
assigned elves a gender based on their first impressions.

"So this elf finds you, tells you to watch xir back
while xe goes through my boat, and offers you two days'
wages? What about the third guy?"

"Didn't know him," he said. "But yeah, that was it.
Xe wanted some backup. Don't know why xe picked us
over anybody else. Xe gave us the guns. I wasn't even
sure the thing worked until I shot at you."

"Any idea where I can find Relict?"

Anzel shook his head. "Never seen xir before.
Probably never will again." He looked at her.

"Are you going to kill me?"

"Should I?" *Please don't give me a reason,* she

thought. She'd killed enough people on this trip already.

"I don't want to die," he said. "I want to forget this ever happened. What the hell am I going to tell her parents?" This brought forth another burst of sobs.

Darsi got up and left the room without another word, taking the wooden box with her.

*   *   *

She went to her tiny quarters, locking the door behind her.

"Grond, you listening?" she said. "I know you bugged the hell out of the boat. This is getting complicated."

She paused, waiting to see if she would get a response.

"Good," she said. "Because I'm handling it. This is still my job, get it?"

She was greeted with additional silence.

Okay, then.

"*Debut*," she said. "Scan the box. Any electronics in there?"

There was a whirr, and a beam of light flickered over the box from two different directions.

BIOLOGICAL MATTER ONLY, the *Debut* answered. AND A FEW NAILS. NOTHING ELECTRONIC.

"I'm not going to like what's inside this box, am I?" she said.

UNABLE TO DETERMINE, the boat answered.

Darsi sighed. If this had been her ship, she'd have made sure the AI had some more personality. Maybe not as much as the *Nameless*, but something.

She dug a claw into a seam and pried the lid off the box.

What she saw inside did not make her terribly happy.

"I knew it," she said.

*   *   *

"*One more question for you," she said*, holding out the object she'd found in the box. "Who's this?"

Anzel *screamed*, trying to shove himself away from the ogre's head she was holding. "I don't know! I've never— " and at that point *completely* lost it, devolving into hoarse screaming, scrabbling with his feet and trying to yank his hands out of the cuffs.

Well. He's not lying, she thought, and went back into her quarters, dropping the head back into the box. It was Fahrhad. It *had* to be Fahrhad. There was no reason for anyone to leave any other ogre heads in her ship.

She paused for a moment, savoring the ridiculousness of having just had that thought.

The kid really was just a hire. He didn't even qualify as *muscle*. He was just a hire.

"I'll be honest. I'm not sure what to do with you," she said, walking back into the room with him. He was wild-eyed, still panicking about the head. "I don't need you deciding you're tough enough to come back and take revenge for your friend. I don't need you deciding you and five or six of your *friends* are tough enough for that. And I don't need this Relict realizing you're a loose end and deciding to take you out, either. I've *already* got one dead body on my conscience today. I don't need another. So you need to disappear. And so do I."

"I won't tell," he said. "I promise."

"You say that *now*," she said. "I even think you mean it. But you don't know. Somebody tough enough to take the head off an *ogre* is out there somewhere. Probably your elf. You gonna stand up to xir when xe comes looking for you?"

Anzel didn't respond.

"Yeah. I didn't think so. You have any way to get offplanet?"

"No," he said. "And I— my family's here, I couldn't—"

Ugh, she thought.

"Disappear," she said. "I don't care how. I'm blowing this berth the second you're gone. And if I ever see you again I'm going to assume you don't have my best interests in mind. Your friend was an accident. You won't be. Clear?"

He shook his head.

She moved behind him, disengaging the cuffs and snapping a tiny tracker under the collar of his jacket as she hauled him to his feet.

"Go," she said. "Come back for the body in a few hours."

"Thank you," he whispered, and fled the boat.

*　　*　　*

True to her word, she took off a few minutes later, putting the *Debut* into low orbit while she thought through her options. Even if the head *wasn't* Fahrhad's, the job was obviously blown. The elf had specifically raided *her* boat, and even if xe had left the head behind by accident, the mere fact that it had been *brought along* spoke volumes. She spent a couple of hours going over the interior of the *Debut* as carefully as she could, running a decontamination routine and making sure nothing else was missing or had been left behind. Along the way, she found two bugs, both with tiny notes attached. One of them said *Good job! Keep looking!* and the other said *Good job! I'm sure this is the last one.* She kept the notes, leaving the bugs behind. Grond had likely stashed one or two behind wall panels somewhere anyway and she didn't feel like literally tearing the ship apart to find them. So long as he didn't try to interfere, she didn't mind him listening in. At least one of the bugs was actually planted right on the control panel for the ship, meaning that he *knew* she was going to find them. He wanted her to know he was listening.

Might be something on the outside of the ship, too. She resolved to go over the ship carefully as soon as she figured out where she could safely land. The good news was that Untkaar didn't appear to be heavily policed. There were plenty of planets where any attempt to land a boat outside of a regulated spaceport would be at least *noticed*, if not acted upon immediately. Untkaar wasn't one of those planets. She just needed a flat, clear area. Preferably two, actually: one to check over the outside of the ship for anything else that wasn't supposed to be there and one to move the ship to after that check was finished.

The only question was what to do after that. The job was blown, and through no fault of hers that she could figure. She'd barely been on-planet long enough to *make* any mistakes. Either someone in her mother's organization or Fahrhad had screwed up, and she had a pretty strong suspicion that it wasn't her mother. She could justify just keeping the package and heading directly back to Arradon.

That was leaving some work incomplete, though. The first thing Rhundi would do when she got back home would be to send Grond and Brazel back to Rainwyr to find out what had happened. *If* she played her cards right, she might be allowed to accompany them, but there was every chance that she'd have to stay behind.

No. She was going to figure this out. She wasn't going to take any stupid risks— there was absolutely *no* chance that she was winning a fight with anyone able to behead an ogre— but if her first mission had been blown she wanted to know why.

She was, at the very least, going to have to go to the damned brothel and ask some questions.

*   *   *

She got lucky— the brothel was in a wooded area, which had made her think it was going to be difficult to find somewhere to put the *Debut*, but there was an acceptable landing spot where the woods gave way to the water a couple of kilometers to the west. She spent an hour climbing all over the ship looking for anything that didn't belong there and didn't find anything. She was going to move the ship, but had a better idea, strapping a remote comm onto her wrist and sending the *Debut* back into low geosynch orbit. It would be fine up there unless someone actually attacked it, in which case the AI was programmed to do everything it could to escape— which was good for the *Debut*, but less good for her, as she'd be stranded on Untkaar until it was safe to bring the boat back down to the surface again.

Maybe she'd steal a ship, if that happened. She'd never done that before. It might be fun.

The last thing she did before sending the boat off was load herself up with every single dangerous thing she'd thought to bring with her. Her staff, half a dozen knives, a couple of flashbangs that she was pretty sure Grond had left behind, and, after thinking about it a bit, the dead girl's gun. She shaved her arms and her eyepatch again and rubbed her skin down with Grond's antiseptic gel, adding an interesting sheen to her bluish skin. Anzel's rifle was a bit too big for her to carry around, but she buried it near the landing zone in case she needed it. She buried Fahrhad's head, too. The package came with her. If it was going to be stolen from her, she was going to see the faces of the people doing it.

She wondered if the name of the brothel really was the *Deep Shaft*.

"Time to find out," she said, and headed off on foot, the sound of the *Debut*'s takeoff roaring behind her.

*   *   *

From the outside, the ogre bar looked almost rustic. The outside was all logs and natural-colored local wood, and the entrance was through saloon-style swinging doors, which were a common affectation in ogre buildings. She could easily have just ducked underneath the door without trying very hard, but she pushed it open anyway.

The inside was completely different. From the outside, she was expecting dirty and smelly. Instead, she got a place that *almost* approached classy, with muted lighting, low music playing, and furniture that looked carefully cared-for. If you overlooked the occasional cage hanging from the ceiling with a gyrating female—

of two or three different species— in it, or the stripper's runway that ran down the middle of the common area, it could be any of the restaurants on Arradon that she'd eaten at. The place smelled bad, but not nearly as bad as she'd expected, and most of the more objectionable smells were coming from the rooms that surrounded the balcony on the open second floor. The sole stairway was at the foot of the runway, spiraling up to the rooms upstairs. The bar took up the entire back wall of the room.

The words *THE SHAFT* were printed on the runway in big letters.

Oh. I never ever wanted to be right about that, she thought, fighting back giggles again and only barely succeeding. *They weren't even bothering to be subtle.* There was no way anyone in here was going to take her seriously if she walked through the door and immediately collapsed on the floor laughing. *Keep it together.*

There were only a handful of patrons in the room, all ogres, plus the bartender. She figured the women in the cages weren't going to be terribly interested in talking to her.

Amazingly, no one even looked her way. She'd tried to prepare for a number of possible reactions to her presence but indifference hadn't been one of them.

Well. To the bar, then. The bartender looked up and made eye contact once she got within a couple of meters, an amused look on his face. He was actually on the small side for a full-blooded ogre, no more than a few centimeters taller than Grond at the most and not as thickly muscled as most ogre males were. He *almost* looked like he might be a halfogre, but the thick brow and slightly protruding lower jaw made that unlikely. He was just one of the smaller ones.

So are you. Don't get cocky.

The most amazing thing about him, though, was his hair. The ogre practically sported a *mane,* with a ridiculous shock of straight black hair spraying in all directions from his scalp and easily halfway down his back. Most ogre males either kept their hair short or shaved their heads. She did a quick scan of the rest of the patrons to see if it was a local style. No one else sported his haircut.

"Drink?" he said.

"Looking for someone," she said, climbing up into a bar stool and not doing a great job of looking suave about it. Seated, her chin barely came up to the bar, so she knelt on the stool. "You know Fahrhad?"

The ogre rumbled, deep in his chest, a flash of red coming over his eyes. Darsi tensed. Red-eyed ogres were *definitely* not something she had been hoping to see. Then he looked at her a bit more closely and the glow faded. His arm shot out, snatching her left wrist. His hand was big enough that he got most of her left hand too. He held her arm out, looking at it carefully.

"Who did the work?" he said.

"Why does it matter?" she asked, wincing as he tightened his grip a bit. There was no way she was going to pull away from him, so she didn't bother trying. She started wondering if she should go for a weapon.

"Ogre work, right?" he said. "He tell you what this says?"

"Says?" she said. The design was mostly geometric, abstract work. It didn't look like language *at all*.

"You got tatted up by a scholar," he said. "There's a couple different references to old myths hidden in there.

Most of us wouldn't even recognize them." He winked at her. "Luckily for you, I read."

Maybe he is *a halfogre,* she thought. "What's it to you, anyway?"

"It's the story of Iklis. I think I'll let him give you the details," the other ogre said. "Just be aware that he made you interesting, and that normally somebody walks in my bar demanding to see my brother, and my brother's been dead for a few days, well, I might wanna beat that person to death just on principle. Those tats let you stay alive long enough to explain yourself."

Iklis. Grond's longbow Angela was an Iklis sniper's longbow. She'd always assumed it was a planet, but she'd never asked him about it.

The bartender let go of her arm.

"So explain, little gnome," he said. "Or maybe I throw you out of my bar, but not until after hanging that arm up above it somewhere. It's good work, after all."

Fahrhad's brother, she thought. *Okay. Let's try this.*

"It's been darker than usual in the mines lately," she said. That was what Farhad was supposed to say to *her.* It was his identification phrase.

The bartender stared at her, his face emotionless. For a moment, neither of them moved.

"The coal absorbs all the light," he said. Darsi relaxed, just the tiniest bit.

"Come with me," he said. "Boksch! Come cover the bar for me. I got a thing here."

Another ogre stood up from a table and headed toward the bar. The bartender turned and headed back toward the kitchens without another word. Darsi followed. He walked into a cramped, brightly-lit office and sat down behind a desk. She decided to stand.

"So show me this package that got my brother killed," he said. "I thought Rhundi was sending us a *human*. What is she, your mom?"

"Yeah," Darsi said.

The bartender laughed. "Grond's work. I shoulda guessed."

"You know Grond, too?"

"Yeah," he said. "Name's Kerron. Now that we're old friends, lemme see the fuckin' box."

She took it out of her pack and put it in front of him. He put a hand on it, and she heard an identcoder inside the box start to spin up. Kerron winced as the box took a blood sample.

And then it simply fell apart.

"Shit," they both said at the same time.

*   *   *

"*Is … is that what I think it is?*" she said.

"Yeah," he said. "What the hell was Fahrhad into?"

"You don't know?" she said. "But the box opened for you."

"Rhundi knows we work as a pair," Kerron said. "She'd have coded it for both of us. But he didn't tell me this was coming, or what he planned to do with it. Did you know he was dead?"

"An elf with a couple of local escorts left his … uh, his *head* in my ship yesterday," she said. "Tried to find the box, too, but didn't end up having time. I got some information out of one of the bodyguards. Xir name is Relict. I think it was xir that killed Fahrhad. I wasn't even sure it was him. My dossier didn't have a description or anything."

"Where's the head?" Kerron said. His eyes were red again, but Darsi didn't think it was for her this time.

"I buried it," she said. "I can show you where."

Kerron nodded. "You know anything about the elf other than xir name?"

"Scars all over xir face," Darsi said. "At least according to the bodyguard. And I don't think xe really needed the backup, either."

"Fuck," Kerron said.

He lifted the Benevolence helmet off the table, looking inside it.

"How much you wanna bet this was the elf's?" he said.

That's trouble, Darsi thought.

"Wait," she said. "Relict *ran away* when I startled xir guards yesterday. Who manages to behead an ogre but runs away from a gnome? Ex-Benevolence shouldn't have been worried about *either* of us. And hiring local kids as lookouts? Why? It doesn't make sense."

"Dunno," Kerron said. "Maybe it's got something to do with the—"

The explosion from the direction of the dance floor cut off anything else he was going to say.

"Stay here," he shouted, eyes blazing red, and stormed out of the room, weapons in both hands. Darsi heard dozens of shots echoing from the front room, along with a chorus of yells and hoarse, deep screams.

She shoved the helmet back into her pack and summoned her ship back from orbit. Then she activated both ends of her staff, following Kerron out of the room.

This is a terrible idea.

She hadn't been sent to Untkaar to fight Benevolence. She'd been sent to Untkaar on a *milk run.*

Milk runs always went bad.

She paused outside the office, trying to decide what to do. The *Shaft* almost certainly had a back exit. She could be out the door in seconds. Or she could join the fight at the front, or at least go *see what was happening*. Kerron was at least nominally on her side. That might not last if she ran away on him.

More bellowing and yelling from the front of the building. But these weren't screams of pain. And the shooting had stopped.

She made her decision and headed toward the bar.

Most of the front room was in flames. At least a couple of the patrons were injured, and one looked dead or close to it. The rest of them were putting fires out.

Kerron and Boksch were enthusiastically beating the living hell out of something on the floor.

By the time she made it over to them, Kerron was standing up straight, one arm shoving Boksch away from whoever they were taking apart.

There was an elf on the ground. Well, *most* of one. It looked like the elf's legs and one arm had been mechanical, and they'd been torn clean off xir body. It was tough to see if xir face had any old scars on it because of all the new blood.

"Is that Relict?" she asked.

"Xe threw an incendiary as soon as xe came in the door," Boksch said. "Blew the runway to hell, killed Oreg. Pointed a gun at me— it's around here somewhere— and then just *collapsed*."

Kerron looked her way. "I got here just as Boksch was jumping on top of xir. Xe never even fought back. How the hell did this thing kill my brother?"

Relict convulsed a few times, spitting a fine mist of

vomit and blood into the air. Darsi turned her head to the side, braced herself, and made sure the elf's airway was clear.

Xir one biological arm was bare. It was covered in scars too, including one huge, prominent one at the shoulder.

"Withdrawal?" Darsi asked. "Is that a thing? My mom's had that helmet for a while. Maybe losing their armor makes them nuts."

"Who the hell knows?" Kerron said. "Let's finish the job and be done with it." The ogre had holstered his guns. He drew one now, pointing it at the elf's head.

"If you kill xir, you'll never know how Fahrhad died, or why," Darsi said.

"He's dead one way or another," Kerron said. "What do I care anymore?"

"You don't want to know why he was taking delivery of a Benevolence helmet from my mother? You're sure about that?"

Kerron put the gun away.

"Tie xir up," he said to Boksch. "Figure out a way. And do something to keep xir from talking. Blindfold, too."

"Ain't that a little overkill?" the other ogre said. "Xe's such a little thing."

"Xe's Benevolence," Kerron said. "Or maybe ex-Benevolence. Take no chances."

He looked at Darsi. "Take the helmet. I'd give you your payment but I don't know what it was. Just take the damn thing and get out of here. I'll deal with ... *that*."

"You don't think that—"

Kerron's eyes went bright red.

"I think I'm done with everything right now. I think

Fahrhad and I came out here to get *away* from this bullshit and I'm not in the fucking mood to see you any more, Iklis tattoos or not. Get outta my whorehouse, gnome."

Darsi nodded. This job was about as blown as it could be. She had no good reason to—

Energy blasts flooded the door. She dove for the floor. Kerron stood in front of her, a confused look on his face.

"What the fuck …" he mumbled, and then crumbled to the floor, a half-dozen smoking holes in his chest.

A thought struck her, and she checked the tracker she'd attached to Anzel's jacket.

The tracker showed him eight meters away. He was either more dangerous an adversary than she'd thought or under some serious compulsion. She'd heard of Benevolence doing things like that before.

Great.

Her subcomm pinged. It was Grond.

"Busy right now," she said, as another volley of bolts flew in through the door. Some of the remaining ogres began firing back, but she was pretty sure they were shooting blind.

"I'm pulling you out," Grond said. "Go out the back. This just got too hot."

"Fuck *that*," Darsi said. "This is just getting *fun*." She cut the connection, not actually feeling her own bravado. But if she let Grond rescue her from this, she'd never be able to go out on a job solo again.

Going out the back was a good idea, though. If only she had brought those goggles, she—

Wait.

She opened her bag and pulled the Benevolence

helmet out again.

Ooooooh, this is a terrible idea. But the thing *had* to have all sorts of visual field enhancements and specialized optics in there.

She pulled the helmet onto her head.

*   *   *

For a moment, there was tremendous pain. That went away quickly, though, and then the entire world slowed down. She felt the helmet reshape itself to better fit the protruding snout of a gnome. Her field of vision went black, then lit back up again with the position of every living thing over a kilo in weight within a hundred meters subtly indicated. One of them was subtly outlined in red. She concentrated on it and the walls of the brothel simply *went away*. Anzel was outside up in a tree, carefully camouflaged, pouring fire in through the door. He had a second rifle set up a few meters away, set to autofire, shooting another energy blast every few seconds through the door to confuse his angles.

Darsi felt that it would be very simple to go outside and simply shoot him out of the tree. Everything was moving so *slowly*. Even the shots from Anzel's rifle seemed to be moving like they were dragging themselves through mud. She grabbed Anzel's original pistol from her hip and danced out the door in between blasts. She could see how he had tried to hide. She even understood how *other* people might not be able to see him where he was. She gave him two shots. The first went through his forehead, the second a few inches farther down, transforming his face into a ruin. His body slid out of the branches and crashed to the ground. A faraway part of her regretted having to kill him. He had been a nice person, she thought. He hadn't deserved to be caught up in all of this.

Then there was the second rifle to deal with. She spun toward it as it fired again, the blast passing harmlessly over one shoulder as her third shot directly hit the muzzle. The gun exploded.

Call home, she thought, or was it the helmet talking to her? She ought to—

She came back to herself for a moment, and shoved the helmet off her head, a sharp screech escaping her throat as the connections between her skull and the helmet were suddenly severed. The thing had already started worming into her brain. If she'd been human or an elf, it would have had her already. The armor was slower to adapt to gnomes, apparently.

Back in the bag. The only question left was whether she was leaving Relict with the ogres or not. The elf wasn't in good health. It was possible xe didn't have a lot of time to live. It was also possible that her mother and their troll Benevolence expert Irtuus-bon could get a *lot* of information out of xir during the time xe had left.

"Grond," she said over subcomm.

"Two minutes," he said.

"We're bringing back a prisoner," she said. "An elf. Possibly ex-Benevolence. My ship or yours?"

"Um," the halfogre said. "I vote neither."

"I wasn't asking," she said. "This is *my* job. If you're going to insist on helping me, you're going to do it on my terms."

There was a brief moment. When the halfogre came back, his tone of voice had changed. She could have sworn he'd been laughing.

"Mine," he said. "I'm in the *Nameless*. Namey's got a berth or two that should be able to keep even an ex-Benevolence elf in check until we get home. And we can probably park your boat in the cargo hold, while we're at it."

"The *Debut* will be landing in a few minutes too," she said. "But a few kilometers away. You're coming straight here? Can the *Nameless* do that?"

THE NAMELESS CAN LAND WHEREVER IT WANTS, Namey said into her ear.

"I didn't know you were listening," she said to the boat.

YUP, it answered.

"Fine. Be ready to leave right away. I'm gonna go get the prisoner, and I don't plan on taking no for an answer." She activated the studs on her electrostaff again. Hopefully Boksch wouldn't want anything to do with Relict at this point anyway.

She walked back into the Shaft.

She was expecting nearly anything. Ogres were not especially known for backing down from fights, but the ogres in this place seemed to mostly be locals, and the local population seemed notably low on warriors. Even an ogre with a desk job could be a formidable opponent, of course, just by virtue of their strength and size, but that didn't mean that they wanted to fight *all* the time.

Did it? She hoped not.

Luckily, everyone was far more concerned with Kerron than they were with either the elf or with Darsi. There were a couple of ogres dragging him back toward the kitchen and Boksch was nowhere to be seen.

Relict was lying facedown on the floor, unbound but also unconscious. Darsi checked xir pulse, wondering if one of the ogres had simply killed xir, and found one: weak and thready, but there.

I need you to really be unconscious, she thought.

The elf's mechanical limbs were scattered all over the bar, and likely contained tracking devices. Darsi thought about scooping them up to give them to Irtuus-bon— there was probably *somewhere* on the new *Nameless* that could keep a signal from getting out— but she dismissed the idea. Too dangerous.

Well, at least an elf missing three of xir limbs wasn't going to *weigh* very much. Darsi worked quickly, first frisking Relict for any hidden weapons and, upon not finding any, scooping the elf up and balancing xir over her shoulder. She staggered for a moment under the weight then stabilized herself and carried xir outside.

The *Nameless* was hanging overhead, just above the treeline. The boat adjusted position slightly, then dropped to the ground, knocking several trees flat along the way but not touching the Shaft. The side cargo door opened, Grond standing just inside, Angela at the ready. Darsi dashed aboard.

"I don't like this," Grond said.

"Yell at me later," Darsi said. "For right now, show me where the infirmary is and let's figure out how to keep xir alive and unconscious."

"Give me that," Grond grunted, taking the body away from Darsi. "You act like you've never been on the damn boat before. Over here." He led her to the infirmary, moving quickly. That was another big difference between this ship and the old *Nameless*. The old one's medbay was basically a couch that swung down from the wall and a small closet. This boat had an actual *infirmary*, with room for more than one person to be hurt and everything. It was practically decadent by comparison.

Grond dropped Relict on a bed in the infirmary and strapped xir down, then pushed a couple of buttons in a wall console and a dome snapped down over the bed.

"Namey, you heard the girl. Healing and unconscious. We can do that for an elf, right?"

PROVIDED THAT THE ELF HAS NO MAGICAL MEANS TO FOOL MY SENSORS, YES, the boat replied. YOU MAY BE AWARE THAT THIS IS THE FIRST BENEVOLENCE AGENT WE HAVE PROVIDED MEDICAL CARE FOR. WE SHOULD HAVE A PARTY.

"Figure out the right drinks and we will," Grond said. "Meantime, lock … hell, lock *everything*. The bed, the infirmary, any doors between the infirmary and us. Xe wakes up and gets out of that bed, I want all the oxygen in the infirmary pumped into the atmosphere and then the room filled with acid. You understand?"

I LACK THE CAPACITY TO—

"I said *do you understand?*"

YES SIR.

Grond turned his attention back to Darsi. "Where's the *Debut*?"

"On its way back to where I left it," she said. "Can we pick it up along the way or do we need to land again?"

"Along the way," Grond said. "C'mon, you're pilot. I don't fit in the damn chair."

"Wait, really?" Darsi said.

"No," Grond said. "But you're in the chair. I'm piloting. May need you to shoot somebody, though." The *Nameless* had been specially outfitted for Brazel and Grond to fly. Grond's seat was behind and above

Brazel's, and Brazel generally flew the ship. Clearly the chair didn't actually matter and either seat could pilot.

They both dropped into their chairs, Darsi securing her pack next to the chair and then adjusting her dad's straps to keep herself in place. "I've still got the package, too, by the way. The guy I was delivering too was dead."

"I know," Grond said. "Listening in, remember?"

"Yeah, and remind me to hit you for that later," she said.

"Am I not *saving your ass* right now?"

"Not really," she said. "I took out the guy shooting at us and captured a Benevolence agent. Have *you* ever captured a Benevolence agent?"

No answer from behind her.

"The *Debut* is incoming," Grond said. "I'm going to lock it down outside the *Nameless* so that we don't have to stay in atmosphere while we dock it. There anything on there you need?"

"No," she said. A few minutes later, she felt a *thunk* as the *Debut* was magnetically locked to the outside of the *Nameless*.

"Once we're clear of the planet, we'll head into tunnelspace," Grond said. "Unless you have any reason to stay in the neighborhood."

"Nothing I can think of," she said. "Our contacts are both dead and as far as I know the person who killed them is on board. Unless you feel like trying to fix an environmental nightmare we can take off."

"Not my problem right now," he said. "What's *as far as I know* mean?"

Darsi outlined the entire story for Grond, filling in all of the details his surveillance had missed.

"So if it *wasn't* Relict who killed Fahrhad, it's a

completely separate party, and that person hasn't had any reason to reveal themselves. I mean, he *was* working out of a brothel. Maybe he's got an angry ex-wife or something. But that doesn't explain why Relict was going to *leave his head in the Debut*. It *had* to have been xir. Otherwise, what, she found it and thought I might want it for my collection?"

Grond snorted. "Okay. I'm convinced. Now explain why xe's on my ship instead of lying on the floor of the Shaft with a hole in xir forehead."

"Because Mom's got a leak somewhere," Darsi said. "I think that helmet's the one *you* found. And Mom didn't bother telling me why she sent me to deliver the thing to Fahrhad, and Fahrhad is too dead to explain why he wanted it *or* why he didn't tell his brother it was coming. Mom thought Kerron was involved or she wouldn't have let him unlock the box. So maybe Fahrhad lied to her about something. Either way, Relict found out from *somebody* that the helmet was heading to Untkaar, and xe obviously wanted it back."

Darsi thought for a few more seconds. "And, honestly, looking at how unhealthy Relict seems to be, xe may have *needed* it back. Taking Fahrhad out may have been taken the last bits of strength xe had left. I ... I put the thing on for a second, during the fight at the Shaft. The rush was *incredible*. Xe may have had just enough juice left to survive a fight with an ogre and then lost it when xe attacked the Shaft the second time. Xe'd already collapsed when the ogres got to xir. Relict hasn't woken up since. We need to know what xe knows."

"Good job," Grond said. "Rhundi made the right call letting you handle this."

Do not smile, Darsi thought, and felt her face

disobeying her. *Do not giggle*, she thought, and only barely won that fight.

The *Nameless* trying to drop out from underneath her as the shields absorbed a hit from *something* wiped the look off her face.

"Namey! What the fuck was that?" Grond shouted.

A SINGLE SPIDERSHIP JUST CAME OUT OF THE PLANET'S SHADOW, the ship responded. IT OPENED FIRE IMMEDIATELY. THAT WAS A MISSILE. SEVERAL MORE INCOMING.

"You didn't see it?"

I HAD TIME TO ACTIVATE AND ANGLE THE SHIELDS PROPERLY. YOU ARE NOT DEAD. MAY WE FIGHT BACK NOW?

"Dars, you're gunner," Grond said. "Tell me *right now* if that's a problem."

"How come there's only one?" she said, bringing up the *Nameless'* combat interface. She'd only simulated ship-to-ship combat a few times, but the *Nameless* was a warship. It technically probably didn't even need her assistance to fight back.

SPIDERSHIP IS UNOCCUPIED, Namey said.

"It's *Relict's*," Darsi said. "It's coming after its owner."

"Blow it out of the sky," Grond said, unbuckling himself. "I'm going to go move that recovery pod into somewhere where xe can't send a signal. There's gotta be some hardware in xir head or something like that. Namey, we don't die until I get back."

ACKNOWLEDGED.

Darsi had already shot down two of the missiles. The third missed as the *Nameless* spun crazily out of its way and the fourth bounced harmlessly off the ship's shields to explode a few kilometers away. A second round of fire incinerated the surviving missile as it attempted to regain a target lock, and Darsi turned her attention to the spidership. Spiderships were standard-issue Benevolence single-passenger fighters. They had eight arms, each of which could either be used for assault or maneuverability, but not both at the same time. This meant that a spidership in evasive mode could be insanely difficult to target but not terribly dangerous, but that one bent on destruction was incredibly formidable.

This one was firing at her with three arms, and was mostly missing the target, the shields soaking up the rest. No further missiles were launched, either. It was using two arms to fly. The others …

Two of the others were *missing*. One hung off the ship, only moving in reaction to the spidership's movement, completely dead.

"The ship's a piece of junk," Darsi said, easily catching it in a target lock. Grond and Brazel had spent their entire careers fleeing at the mere *thought* of a Benevolence spidership being nearby. And she was about to destroy one on her first mission.

The *Nameless'* guns erupted, and the spidership was reduced to powder. A few moments later, Darsi felt the entire boat shudder as they leapt into tunnelspace. Short of a blockship between them and Arradon, they were safe for a while.

"Grond?" she said over shipwide comm. "I got it. Everything okay back there?"

"Yeah," he said. "Your buddy had a seizure when xir ship died. The capsule's trying to contain it. I'm putting xir in a shielded berth until we're home. Any more surprises?"

"We're in tunnelspace, if you didn't notice." The feeling of shifting into and out of tunnelspace was pretty subtle so long as you were doing it on purpose. If Grond was distracted with Relict, he likely hadn't felt it.

"Thanks," the halfogre responded. "Go find a bunk and relax. I think you've earned it."

Darsi started to unbuckle herself from the pilot's seat, then stopped.

Nah.

She would stay a pilot a while longer. It was a feeling she wanted to get used to.

*   *   *

INHERITANCE

"*Explain this to me one more time,*" Rhundi said. She rubbed her temple as she said it. There was a headache of rather epic proportions coming on, and this job sounded complicated.

"I need you to find an urn," the dwarf sitting across from her said. His name was Xyl. Usually male dwarves who escaped the matriarchy changed their names. This one, for whatever reason, hadn't.

"One urn," Rhundi said.

"Yes. About half a meter high," he replied.

"And this urn is located where?"

"I have rough coordinates," he said.

"How rough?"

"I can pin it down to a system. I think."

"You *think* you can pin down the location of an object the size of my head to somewhere in an *entire system.*"

"That's correct," he said. Xyl was the first dwarven male Rhundi had ever met who she could use the word *smarmy* to describe. This was new.

"And what's in the urn?"

"The cremains of my mother, Starlight-in-the-Darkness, and my grandmother, Color-of-Rushing-Water."

"And you want to pay me to help you find those cremains," she said. "This is the part where you need to provide me more detail."

"My money isn't good enough?" he asked.

Rhundi glared at him, altering her tone. "You're in *my* office on *my* planet right now, asking for *my* help. I don't need you or have any reason to care what happens to you, and I suspect *someone* very much wants you returned to the fold. You will show me more respect or I will have my employees return you to the nearest dwarf planet. Quite possibly in chains."

Xyl held her gaze for a moment longer, then lowered his eyes. "I apologize," he said. "I need your help. I am doing a poor job of asking for it."

"You are, yes," she agreed. "Answer all my questions and I will consider forgiving you for it. I don't believe a rogue male is simply interested in retrieving the ashes of his ancestors. There is something else going on here. Tell me what it is."

"There is something else in the urn," he said.

"Now we're getting somewhere," Rhundi said. "And that is?"

"A nanocloud that unlocks a vault."

"And in the vault?"

"Enough wealth to buy a small planet."

Rhundi's headache disappeared.

"Keep talking," she said.

"My grandmother was ... *fertile*," he said. "Or at least very interested in a large family. You probably already know that wealthy dwarves rarely actually gestate their children inside their own bodies. My grandmother was no exception, and her wealth gave her ... well, I'll say more *opportunities* than most. My mother has twenty-four sisters and another twenty-five brothers, one to serve as seneschal for each of the sisters. Those twenty-four sisters have a hundred and seven offspring. Of those, fifty-six are female and I believe there are at least two other rogue males. Which means that there are at *least* 83 other people searching for the urn. As one of the rogue males, you can easily imagine that I am *not* interested in being located by my aunts or my cousins. So I need ... well, we'll say *agents* to do the search for me."

"And you don't think showing up with the nanocloud to unlock the vault will lead to trouble?"

"On the contrary, I'm certain it will," he said. "But the cloud will adapt its sequence to the first of us to touch it. Which means that if I reach it first, *no one* in my family can take it from me or open the vault with it. That buys me some leverage."

"This is a ridiculous way of handling an inheritance, you know," Rhundi said.

"Grandmother was eccentric, and mother more so," he said. "My mother was the oldest and should have expected to inherit nearly everything anyway. I think she only went along with Grandmother's wishes because she thought she would outlive the old woman and could simply take the cloud for herself. Instead, they both died in the same raid. And it is not all of her fortune. Just enough to ensure that whoever finds it controls the lineage."

Xyl sat up in his chair and steepled his fingers under his chin. "I would *very much* like to be the one who controls the lineage. I suspect you understand why."

"I do," Rhundi said. "Give my secretary the details of the location and ask him to set you up with a suite for the next few weeks. We will see what we can do for you."

"I thank you," the dwarf said, standing up and bowing.

*   *   *

APPROACHING THE 5254SDO SYSTEM, the Nameless *said as it slipped out of tunnelspace.* Dwarves were notoriously unsentimental about place names, and only the oldest of their planets had names that most of the Known Races would recognize as "normal." Xyl had identified a planet in this system as being a possible location for the urn, so Brazel and Grond headed there first.

"What are we looking at?" Grond asked.

"Six planets in the system," Brazel answered. "Two gas giants, three terrestrials, and an iceball too small and far away to matter. The third terrestrial is the only one worth living on; that's 5254SDO-3. Somewhere in this mess is a very tiny object moving very quickly that we've been hired to locate. Care to speculate on how we're going to do that?"

FOUND IT, Namey said.

Grond started laughing. "Well, that was easy. Can we go home now?"

"And *how* did you find it?" Brazel asked.

THERE ARE CURRENTLY TWO DOZEN SHIPS OF DWARVEN MAKE IN ORBIT OR NEAR PROXIMITY TO 5254SDO-5. I THINK IT IS REASONABLE TO BELIEVE THEY ARE SEARCHING FOR THE URN OR HAVE ALREADY FOUND IT AND ARE COMPETING TO CAPTURE IT.

"Any of them seem to have noticed us yet?"

NO. THEY APPEAR TO BE CHASING SOMETHING IN ORBIT AROUND THE PLANET.

"Chasing? Match velocity and pull up alongside. Easy. How fast is the thing moving?"

IT APPEARS TO BE PLAYING KEEPAWAY.

"Did the dwarf mention the urn being *powered?*" Brazel asked.

HE DID NOT.

Grond was still laughing. "So we need to grab a piece of ceramic moving, what, a few thousand kilometers an hour, that keeps changing direction whenever anyone gets close to it, and we need to do it with *how* many other ships trying to grab it at the same time?"

TWENTY-FOUR PRECISELY. CORRECTION: TWENTY-THREE. THEY HAVE BEGUN SHOOTING AT EACH OTHER.

"So much for family," Grond said.

"It wouldn't surprise me if they all hate each other," Brazel said. "Throwing the majority of your clan's wealth to the winner of a contest is not the action of a family-oriented matriarch. That's vicious."

"So you're splitting everything evenly when you and Rhundi die, huh?"

Brazel grinned. "If only because Darsi would *eat* all

of her siblings if we tried to pull a move like this. It's no fun when there's no contest."

"There's a reason she's my favorite," Grond said.

TWENTY SHIPS REMAINING. THE COMBAT IS SPREADING.

"You're kidding," Brazel said. "Can we get it on viewscreen?"

The viewscreen zoomed into a close-up of 5254SDO-3, and Brazel and Grond watched as a cloud of angular dwarven boats blew the hell out of each other.

"I pick that one," Grond said, highlighting one of the ships. "It's the biggest. Looks heavily armed."

"I pick this one," Brazel said, pointing at a single ship that had pulled out of the combat entirely. "Smart enough to back off and let everybody else destroy each other. Either that or—"

The ship disappeared from the viewscreen.

YOUR CHOICE HAS JUMPED TO TUNNELSPACE, Namey said.

"Think she's got the urn?" Grond said.

"Roll the video back a couple of minutes," Brazel said. "Highlight that one boat. Where's it go?"

The two watched as the ship, initially toward the front of the pack, dove underneath the explosion caused by the first hostilities. It juked to the right, slowed down for a moment, then abruptly wheeled and left orbit.

"It left before the rest of the shooting started," Brazel said. "And nobody noticed because everyone else joined in so fast."

"They've got the damn urn," Grond said.

"Namey, figure out where they went," Brazel said. "And follow them. We're faster than that boat, aren't we?"

PROBABLY, Namey said, his engines powering up.

*　　*　　*

They spent only a few minutes in tunnelspace before the Nameless *suggested exiting.*

THE OUTERMOST PLANET IN THE 5254SDO SYSTEM IS PRECISELY ALONG THE PATH THEY CHOSE, Namey said. AND IT IS FAR ENOUGH FROM THE STAR THAT IT IS REASONABLE TO HAVE JUMPED TO REACH IT.

"Get some distance from it," Brazel said. "I'd prefer they not notice us right away if we can avoid it."

UNDERSTOOD. A moment later, Brazel felt the telltale shimmer in his bones as the boat dropped out of tunnelspace.

FOUND THEM, Namey said. THE SHIP IS IN LOW ORBIT AROUND 5254SDO-6.

"Why stop?" Grond said. "Why not take the thing straight back home?"

"Xyl said that there were other rogues looking for the urn," Brazel said. "Maybe those guys aren't dwarves. The boat *looks* dwarven, though."

"Loaner ship, maybe?" Grond said. "There's no reason—"

There was a flash on the viewscreen, and the ship began noticeably listing to one side.

"That's not good," Grond said.

"Hail them," Brazel said. "Find out what happened."

THEIR SYSTEMS ARE COMPLETELY NEUTRALIZED, Namey said. NAVIGATION, LIFE SUPPORT, COMMUNICATIONS, EVERYTHING. THE SHIP IS CAUGHT IN 5254SDO-6's GRAVITY.

IT WILL CRASH BEFORE WE REACH IT.

"Is it going to survive descent?" Brazel asked.

PROBABLY, Namey said. DWARVEN SHIPS TEND TO BE ROBUSTLY BUILT.

"Get there," Brazel said. "As quick as you can. Does that iceball have an atmosphere?"

NO, Namey said.

"So we've just got the *crash* part to worry about. Move," Brazel said. "Grond, let's get suited up. We're looking for survivors first, then the urn."

The two of them headed to their quarters.

*   *   *

True to the Nameless' *predictions, the ship crashed several minutes before they were able to reach it.* Luckily, external scans indicated that it had managed to land somewhere relatively soft and had sustained surprisingly little damage from the crash.

"Weak gravity," Brazel said. "Lucky for them."

The *Nameless* put down on a flat patch of ice half a kilometer from the crash site. It sunk a meter or two into the surface, then rested on something more solid.

CORRECTION, Namey said. THE PLANET HAS AN ATMOSPHERE. IT IS CURRENTLY FROZEN, HOWEVER. WE JUST LANDED IN IT.

"Explain," Brazel said.

IT IS WINTER IN THIS HEMISPHERE, Namey said. THE ATMOSPHERE IS MOSTLY NITROGEN. IT IS TOO COLD FOR THE NITROGEN TO REMAIN GASEOUS.

"I am suddenly much less excited than I was about walking to that shipwreck," Grond said.

"The suits can handle it," Brazel said.

"The nitrogen snow is *over your head*," Grond said. "It's almost over *mine*. And I don't know about you, but I didn't bring my snowshoes."

"Shit," Brazel said. "Namey, how close can we get?"

MUCH CLOSER, the ship said. AND THE HEAT FROM THE CRASH AND THE LANDING WILL TEMPORARILY SUBLIMATE MOST OF THE SNOW.

"Do it," Brazel said.

*   *   *

"*I'm proud of you,*" Brazel said.

"And why is that?" Grond asked, making the last adjustments to his envirosuit.

"We're on an iceball and you're not griping about it," the gnome replied. Grond had always hated cold.

"I like money, and for once this isn't your fault," Grond said. "It's not like you personally decided to bring us here. That said, let's get this the hell over with."

Brazel pushed a button and the airlock door slid open. The pair felt the blast of cold even through their envirosuits, and there was already snow falling as the atmospheric gases re-froze. The dwarven ship, an unsightly rectangle that looked to be mostly engine, was dug into a rapidly-resolidifying trench a few meters away. Luckily, the entry hatch was still exposed.

"Any life signs on the ship?" Grond asked.

ONE, Namey said. THERE IS A HULL BREACH. THE SHIP IS LOSING PRESSURE RAPIDLY.

"Let's move, then," Brazel said. "That means they lost some people. The boat's too big for a single pilot."

"I take it that means we're using the fast way on the airlock," Grond said.

"Ship's already crashed," Brazel said. "And they're already running out of air. No need to be delicate." The slow way was carefully hacking past the door's security or disabling the lock. The faster way was to just blow the hell out of the thing.

Grond nodded and opened fire on the airlock. A few shots from his heavy pistol melted the locking mechanism into slag, and the halfogre tore the door from its frame before the metal had time to cool back down again.

Brazel moved inside. The inside airlock was closed but not locked. "Lucky," he said. There ship was already losing atmosphere; there was no reason to make it worse.

THE LAYOUT OF THE SHIP IS STANDARDIZED, Namey said. THE LIFE SIGN IS IN THE COCKPIT.

Standard dwarven layout meant a cargo hold in the back between the engines with maintenance spaces on either side, a central corridor flanked by crew spaces— probably with common areas on the left and some number of bunks on the right— and a central cockpit/bridge at the front of the ship. Brazel and Grond turned left, heading for the cockpit.

Grond turned on his external speakers. "STAND DOWN!" he shouted, his amplified voice echoing throughout the boat. "WE'RE NOT HOSTILES. THIS IS A RESCUE OPERATION."

"Hope they're paying attention," Brazel said.

The cockpit door was locked and windowless, with no indication of what might be on the other side. Grond knocked loudly a few times. The two of them listened carefully, but there was no sign of any movement or sound from the other side.

"Break it," Brazel said. Grond shot the lock out and then pried the door open, straining against the first few inches until its internal mechanisms broke and the door flew out of the way. Brazel led the way inside, pistol in hand.

There were three dwarves inside the cockpit: a female and two males. The female was still alive, but unconscious. A knot was already forming on her forehead. She'd probably been bounced around pretty hard during the crash.

The males were dead.

They looked as if they had been dead for *weeks*. Both bodies were half-rotten, a pool of unidentifiable fluids around each of them. One was sitting in the pilot's chair. The second lay in the corner of the room, clearly tossed there by the crash.

"Oooh, that's not good," Grond said.

"Is the urn in here?" Brazel asked. Moving quickly, he put a portable oxygen supply over the survivor's mouth and nose.

Grond looked around. "I don't see it— wait," he said, moving the corpse in the corner out of the way.

"Don't touch the body," Brazel said.

"I'm not," Grond said, holding on to what looked like a clean part of the dwarf's suit. "This one's dressed for a spacewalk. He musta grabbed the urn by hand. That's impressive."

"She let a *male* do that?" Brazel said.

"The other male's the pilot," Grond said. "This is one of the other rogues. It's gotta be." Underneath the body was a small capsule made of ceramic and glass. There had been a lid at one point, but it was missing. Grond picked it up.

"Empty," he said. "There's not even any residue in here."

"Then it never even *had* any ashes in it," Brazel said.

"Take it or leave it?" Grond said.

"Leave it," Brazel said. "It killed those two. No way they died in the crash and ended up looking like *that*. Let's get the hell out of here. You wanna carry her?"

Grond shrugged and picked up the survivor, draping her over a shoulder. "She gonna survive outside?"

"We have to move fast," Brazel said. "If there's cold-weather gear on this boat anywhere I wouldn't know where to find it. Much more than a few seconds outside will probably kill her."

"Let's check the crew cabins," Grond said. "If they knew to come to this system they might have come prepared to land here."

Brazel headed for the berths while Grond hauled the unconscious dwarf toward the airlock.

"Good call," the gnome said over comm. "There's a set right here. It'll take a minute to figure out how to set all the seals, but—"

FOUR SHIPS INCOMING, Namey said. I WOULD SUGGEST HURRYING.

"We stuff her in it and hope she doesn't die," Grond said. "Get here."

Brazel hauled the empty snowsuit toward his partner, and the two of them wrapped the dwarf in it as best they could and Grond wrapped his arms around her, holding her to his chest in hopes that his own cold-weather gear would shield her from the elements They bolted out of the airlock, leaving the bodies and the capsule behind.

There was already nearly a meter of snow outside, and visibility was nearly nothing.

"Hit the engines, Namey," Brazel said. "We're blind out here."

Grond switched his grip on the dwarf, holding her under one arm, and grabbed Brazel with the other, depositing the gnome unceremoniously on top of his shoulders. There was a loud hissing sound as the *Nameless* ignited its engines and the snow turned back to gas again. Moments later, the three of them were on the ship.

"Get her to the medbay," Brazel said. "And then get ready for whatever's next."

Calling what the *Nameless* had a "medbay" was perhaps overstating things, but Grond was able to get the dwarf secured and on an IV drip within a few minutes. The drip would keep her unconscious and begin repairing any injuries that she might have. If anything was broken, they could set that later. The boat would keep her stable until they got somewhere more advanced. He finished setting her up and headed for the copilot's seat in his quarters. His viewscreen was ominous, as the *Nameless* showed four hostile ships in what looked very close to combat range.

"You in?" Brazel said over the ship comm.

"Go," Grond said, and his seat kicked him in the back as Namey took off.

WE ARE BEING HAILED.

"Bring it up," Brazel said, and a holographic image of a very irritated-looking dwarven woman appeared in front of him and Grond.

"Who the hell are you?" the dwarf asked.

THE SIGNAL IS BEING SENT FROM THE LEAD

SHIP, Namey said.

"Who the hell are *you*?" Brazel asked. "We're investigating a crash. We're being helpful."

"No one asked you to be helpful," the other dwarf spat.

"Isn't that what distress signals are usually for?"

"Leave the system now," she answered. "This is our business."

OTHER SHIPS IN THE SYSTEM ARE HEADED OUR WAY, Namey chimed in. WE HAVE BEEN NOTICED.

"Not now," Brazel hissed, breaking the ship-to-ship comm for a moment. "There was no one alive on that ship," he said to the dwarf. "The cockpit was crushed. No survivors."

"I don't think I believe you," the dwarf said.

"Look, we don't need to get involved in whatever dispute you ladies are having," Brazel said. "You go right ahead and explore that ship. You'll see we're telling the truth. We'll just be on our way—"

The *Nameless'* shields flared into life as the lead dwarven skiff opened fire.

"We running or fighting?" Grond shouted.

"Both!" Brazel answered, flipping the *Nameless* out of the way of the oncoming ships and speeding off.

At least dwarven ships usually aren't that fast, he thought. That lead ship looked pretty deluxe, though. It was twice the size of the other two and looked ten times as expensive. Other ships started to pop onto the viewscreen as more and more of their pilots realized something interesting was happening at the outskirts of the system.

Meanwhile, Grond opened fire, stressing the lead

ship's shields. One of the backups strayed into the field of fire and caught a lucky shot directly to the engines, spinning down into 5254SDO-6.

"That one doesn't count!" Brazel yelled. "You didn't shoot him! He just flew into the lasers!"

Grond laughed. "He's gone, ain't he?"

The *Nameless* was already starting to leave the two remaining smaller ships in the distance. Grond tasked a missile to each of them and focused his attention on the lead ship. Getting a lock-on was difficult, as both ships were ducking and weaving as quickly as they could and the other boat's shields appeared to be a bit stronger than theirs were.

"Just slow them down," Brazel said. "We're getting out of here as quick as we can. Namey, *any* system. I don't care which one. Just get out of here. *Fast.*" He headed for the outskirts of the system. Getting as far away from 5254SDO-6's gravity well would help with a rapid jump to tunnelspace.

The *Nameless* lurched as a missile exploded nearby— a close miss, but enough to rock the ship. Grond cursed and shot back, overpowering another ship's shields and causing enough damage that it pulled out of the fight. The capital ship continued to close on them, but it was now fending off attacks from other dwarven ships as well.

"I'd like to point out that I said this was the ship that was going to win the fight," Grond said.

Brazel blinked. "You're about to be blown into a cloud of atoms and you're being *smug?*"

A few shots got through the other ship's shields, tracing a scar across its surface.

"Never a bad time to be smug," Grond replied. A

moment later, he and Brazel felt the telltale shudder as the *Nameless* jumped into tunnelspace.

"Ought to be safe for a few minutes," Brazel said. "Namey, I want three or four jumps in random directions then start getting us home. Kill a few hours leaping around, though; let's not make it easy to follow us."

ACKNOWLEDGED, the boat said.

*   *   *

"So," Brazel said to the dwarf as she slowly awakened. "You have some explaining to do." It had taken longer for her to come to consciousness than he expected. The *Nameless* was returning to Arradon through tunnelspace, and no trace of dwarven pursuit had been discovered. As far as any of them could tell, they'd gotten away clean, at least for now.

The dwarf fixed one eye on Brazel. The other didn't seem entirely interested in opening just yet. She was young; younger than Brazel would have expected, to be out actively competing for her grandmother's inheritance. Her beard had been growing in, but she'd trimmed it down, and not carefully, either. It wasn't a style choice he'd seen from many dwarves. Then again, she'd let one of the male dwarves pilot her ship, too. Something odd was definitely going on.

"Where 'm I?" she mumbled.

"Safe, for now," Brazel said. "Your ship crashed. We saved you."

She coughed. "Brothers?"

Brazel thought about that for a moment. *Her first priority was to ask about her brothers. Interesting.*

"They didn't make it," Brazel said. The dwarf closed

her eyes again, punching a fist into the webbing of the cot she was lying on.

"I'm sorry, if that matters to you at all," he added.

"Are you taking me back?" she asked, sounding defeated. A few weak coughs escaped her chest.

"Right now we're just taking you with us," Brazel said. "Until we decide what to do with you. That's up in the air right now."

A harder coughing fit hit her, and Brazel fit an oxygen mask over her face.

"Just breathe for a few minutes," he said. "Don't try to talk." Then, addressing the *Nameless*: "How's she look, anyway?"

HER VITALS ARE STABLE, the boat responded. SHE APPEARS TO HAVE SOME FOREIGN MATERIAL IN HER LUNGS. THAT IS THE CAUSE OF THE COUGH. VERY LITTLE IN THE WAY OF INJURIES. IT IS SURPRISING THAT SHE WAS NOT MORE SERIOUSLY HURT IN THE CRASH. The bruise on her head was mottled, but already less livid than it had been when they'd found her.

The dwarf lay still for a few minutes, breathing deeply, then sat up a bit and removed the mask.

"My name is Dust-of-the-Plains," she said. "I'm guessing you know why my ship crashed."

"We have an inkling," Brazel said. "Or, at least, we have an inkling of what you were doing out there."

"That goddamned urn," Dust-of-the-Plains said. "Pride-of-the-Abandoned was convinced it would solve all of his problems in life. Told him it wouldn't." She coughed again, a trace of red coming away on the brown skin of her hand as the fit stopped. "What happened to our ship?"

"*Our* ship?" Brazel asked.

"We don't all think like our mothers," she snapped. "Pride-of-the-Abandoned and Nyd were my protectors when I was growing up. My friends. My *only* friends. None of my sisters or my mother or my grandmother really wanted anything to do with me. Yeah, it was *our* ship. Not mine."

Brazel backed away a bit, raising his hands in apology. "Whatever you want," he said. "It's none of my business. You've got to admit, though, it's not the way things are usually done with you folk."

Dust-of-the-Plains sneered. "That's the idea," she said. "Where *is* the urn, anyway?"

"Underneath your brother's body," Brazel said. "We're pretty sure whatever was in the urn was what killed the two of them. Was Pride-of-the-Abandoned the one who went out and snagged the thing?"

"That was Nyd," she said. "Pride-of-the-Abandoned was the pilot. What do you mean it killed them? Our *ship crashed*."

"You seem to have cared about your brothers," Brazel said. "You may want to wait a bit before I tell you about this. Get your head together."

"Don't patronize me, gnome," she said.

Brazel nodded. "Fine. Whatever the shit was in the urn, it practically *melted* both of them. They looked like they'd been dead for weeks, and dead in a humid, hot climate, for that matter, and not on a boat that had crashlanded into an iceball. We *probably* ought to have you in quarantine. I think whatever it was killed Pride-of-the-Abandoned *hard*, enough that he dumped the ship into a death spiral toward the planet that the AI couldn't compensate for. Or maybe something in there went after the *ship*, too."

He stared off into space for a moment. "Shit. We really should have thought of that before we let you on board."

"We were in a bit of a hurry," Grond said from behind him. The halfogre had managed to make it into the medbay without Brazel hearing him coming. Nothing as big as he was had any right to be that *quiet*. Grond snuck up on people all the time without even trying.

Dust-of-the-Plains started laughing, only stopping when another coughing fit forced her to.

"Not the reaction I thought that news was going to get," Brazel said.

She coughed again a few times. "You don't know me," she said. "I thought something like this was going to happen. The story about the urn was a lie. Should have known when the older sisters didn't head out looking for it. The whole damned thing was a honeypot. She wanted to kill off the males and the rogues. That's what it was about." She pounded a fist into her chest a few times.

"And you watch. Your ship said I had something in my lungs? They're full of nanoparticles. I'm a walking goddamned bomb. I'd bet my entire generation's share of the inheritance that as soon as I get near another male I'm related to the cloud will blow me open to get to him."

She collapsed back into her cot.

"I'm fucked," she said. "She won."

She laughed again.

"Makes me wonder if Color-of-Rushing-Water and Starlight-in-the-Darkness are even *dead*. This is the sort of thing my grandmother would love to watch. The old hag is probably laughing her ass off somewhere."

"So what do we do about it?" Grond asked. He exchanged a look with Brazel, leaving the question *And who's going to be paying us for this?* unspoken.

*   *   *

Very few dwarves lived on Arradon, and only two or three kept lodgings at Rhundi's resort, so once her engineers had scanned the *Nameless* every way they could think of and determined that the ship wasn't harboring anything that could harm any of their guests they were allowed to land. Dust-of-the-Plains was quickly stuffed into an isolation suit and hustled away to the quarantine wing of the resort's medical facilities, where gnomish doctors and tech staff poked and prodded and scanned her, trying to figure out if the nanoparticles could be deactivated or cured and if they were likely to become active again anytime soon. This spurred any number of lively arguments, including whether the word "deactivated" or "cured" was the right one to describe what they were trying to do.

"Sooner or later, we'll have to tell Xyl we're back," Brazel said. He and Rhundi sat in her office, remotely observing Rhundi's medical and engineering staff do their jobs.

"Dust-of-the-Plains hasn't asked for him, and he's not pushing for status updates," Rhundi said. "We'll tell him when we have something to tell him. Do you think we ought to bring Irtuus-bon into this? It's been a few days. My girls don't seem to be getting anywhere."

"He specializes in Benevolence tech," Brazel said. "You think that's what this is? Color-of-Rushing-Water was an asshole, but I don't see her dabbling in that kind of technology. Have you ever known *any* dwarves who collaborated with Benevolence?"

"Only a couple, and they were stooges," Rhundi said. "But the tech's clearly something my people haven't seen before, and I'd like to know who this stuff is programmed to kill before we let anyone leave the planet." She thought for a moment more. "If we can even *let* them leave. Irtuus-bon might be able to help."

"What's the down side, then?" Brazel asked.

"My staff hates him," she said. "That, and do you *really* want Irtuus-bon to have access to anything more dangerous than the stuff he's already meddling with?" The troll had amassed a small collection of Benevolence artifacts and weaponry when Rhundi met him, most of which was now locked away out of his immediate access. He was known to occasionally be a bit forgetful, and concern for the lives of those around him was not always one of his highest priorities.

"So have them bring some of the particles to him," Brazel said. "What's the worst that can happen?"

"Planetary extinction via grey nanotech sludge," Rhundi responded promptly.

Brazel thought about it for a moment.

"There's other planets," he said. "Let's try it out."

*   *   *

It took four more days to puzzle the technology out, and Irtuus-bon was much more willing than usual to share the credit once they found a breakthrough. The troll sat in Rhundi's office, his tall frame folded into Grond's chair, a lead box in his lap.

"This is … *extraordinarily* dangerous," Irtuus-bon

said. "Are we ... giving it back?"

"We are not," Rhundi said. Irtuus-bon made a little mewl of pleasure and cradled the box closer to his chest. Rhundi took a moment to enjoy the feeling of her skin crawling underneath her fur and then shook it off and moved on. Sirrys ban Irtuus bon Alaamac was a phenomenal intellectual talent, but occasionally he was *immensely* creepy.

"Tell me exactly what it is," she said.

"It is precisely what we thought it was," he responded. "The nanoparticles are ... keyed to the DNA of the males from Color-of-Rushing-Water's line. In fact, they appear to be from at least a generation *older* than Color-of-Rushing-Water. When they come in contact with a being possessing the targeted genetics, they activate."

"And that activation does what?"

The troll giggled. "It *eats* the genetic material, and begins using it to reproduce itself. The results ... would look much like what Grond and Brazel reported aboard the ship. It then searches out nearby hosts that do *not* possess the target DNA, and deactivates for a time."

"For a time?"

Irtuus-bon nodded.

"Your gnomes discovered this, not I. There is a timing function built in. If the nanoparticles are not expressed out of the bodies of their hosts within a certain amount of time ... they eat the host as well, and spread themselves again. Dust-of-the-Plains was ... nearer to death than she realized."

"Can they get out of that box?"

"We have deactivated the timer," Irtuus-bon said. "We have no reason to believe that the nanoparticles ...

can adapt themselves to nonorganic matter. But there is more."

Rhundi waited.

Irtuus-bon continued to stare at her silently.

"You're going to make me say it, aren't you?" she said. "Fine. *What more?*"

"We know how to reprogram the genetic strings," Irtuus-bon said. "We can target ... *anyone* with this. Or anything."

Rhundi's blood went cold.

"You understand that I can't let you keep that," she said.

The troll's body underwent a brief shudder, collapsing into a shorter, wider form, then— with some apparent effort— restoring himself to his usual shape.

"We ... understand," he said, elongating his arms to deposit the box on Rhundi's desk next to her. "We may wish to investigate further in the future, of course."

"Of course," Rhundi said. "Under the terms of your contract. I won't be handing you something this dangerous just because you're bored. But thank you. You did good work. Do I need to give bonuses to any of my other scientists for putting up with you for this long?"

Irtuus-bon considered this idea for a few seconds.

"I do not believe so," he said. "There was ... much less yelling, this time, than the last time we worked together."

"Good," Rhundi said, making a mental note to distribute bonuses anyway. "Send Gorrim in on your way out, would you?"

Irtuus-bon nodded and stood, leaving the room quietly. Rhundi considered the box on her desk carefully.

I should probably have this destroyed on the spot, she

thought. But if the dwarves had access to this technology, that probably meant that it was more widespread than she realized. And she was loath to ever get rid of a weapon.

"Tell the dwarves they can finish out the week at the resort, rent-free," she told Gorrim as he entered her office. "Tell Xyl we weren't able to solve his problem for him. Have the doctors look Dust-of-the-Plains over one more time. And then make sure they get the hell out of here."

Gorrim nodded, turning to leave the room.

"And get Brazel for me, too," she said to her secretary's back. "Tell him I've got something he needs to find a hiding place for."

*   *   *

THE RECRUIT

"That chunk of space is just full *of pirates, you know.* We've had to start routing through the Yngrasar system. You'll get a bonus if you manage to get the shipment there early, but if you lose the whole thing … probably better if you don't even try."

"I will manage," the elf said. "My ship is fast and well-armed. I have little fear of pirates."

The dwarf shrugged, running a hand through her beard. "Your loss if you get hit. You've got plenty of time to go the long way around. It's not like the hardware you're moving is going to go bad or anything."

"I understand," the elf said. "I'm eager to get moving. What else do I need to do to claim the shipment?"

"Retinal scan and a thumbprint," the dwarf said. "What was your name again?"

"Asper," xe said, and pressed xir thumb to the scanner.

*   *   *

It took only a day to locate the pirates. Faster than Asper had expected. Whoever they were, they were getting braver, as Asper hadn't even reached the point where the "safe" route diverged from the route cutting through the pirate lanes. The *Shield and Spear's* long-range scanner package— a present from Lady Remember herself— detected the blockship just before xe entered its range, and Asper was able to brace for the soul-deep tearing feeling that came with being pulled from tunnelspace involuntarily.

Interesting, xe thought, observing the blockship. It hadn't been that long since blockships were Benevolence-only technology. Xe'd heard stories that at least one of them had been stolen. Clearly at some point someone had reverse-engineered it, because the ungainly mess in the distance in front of the *Shield and Spear* was clearly not of Benevolence make. It had the cobbled-together, built-from-spare-parts look that xe would expect from technology that had been stolen and then built in secret and on the cheap.

In other words, it was *exactly* what xe was looking for.

WE ARE BEING HAILED, the *Shield and Spear* AI said.

"Go ahead."

The voice on the other end was human, and sounded positively jubilant.

"Now, I'm just betting that *someone* warned you that

cutting through this part of space was a terrible idea," he said. "And you didn't listen. Why didn't you listen? Because now you have to turn over everything you're transporting. And probably your ship, too. It looks expensive."

Yes, this was certainly exactly what xe had been looking for.

A few seconds of silence passed before the voice began speaking again. "Nothing to say, eh? That's fine. Power down your ship, deactivate any weapons, and prepare to be boarded. We outnumber you, so no silly moves like trying to fight your way out of this. It's happening. Let's try and get this over with without anybody getting killed, okay? I'm going to interpret further silence as compliance."

A quick sensor sweep indicated four mid-range fighters hiding behind the blockship. Newer models, but nothing xe couldn't handle. But the blockship wasn't a place to live. There had to be some sort of base nearby.

Also good. Asper complied with the pirate's orders and brought shields and weapons down. It made little difference; they could be powered back up again in milliseconds if the ship AI detected an attack. No need for the pirates to know that, though.

"Good," the voice said. "We're on our way. How many of you are there? No being quiet, now. We expect an answer."

"One," xe said. "I'm the only person on board."

"Good, good. You sit tight now. We'll be there in a moment."

Asper disengaged all the internal locks on the boat and moved to the airlock. Xe put on a cloak that concealed xir form underneath it, but kept the hood down. If the pirates had any sense at all they would pat xir down before allowing xir off the *Shield and Spear,* so xe wore two weapons: a pistol in an ankle holster and one other, much more carefully concealed. The pistol, of course, would be found. The other was much less likely.

The pirates only sent three over, two human males and a female dwarf. The dwarf did all the talking.

"I'm flying your ship. You're going with these two," she said, cocking a thumb over her shoulder at the humans. "Any lockouts or anything else I need to know about getting this thing moving?"

"Nothing," Asper said.

"No stupid surprises you have stashed anywhere? Because whatever happens to me happens to you, y'know."

Asper only nodded.

"Smart move. The boat might be yours, but I bet the cargo isn't. No use dying for someone else's money. Check xir over," the dwarf said, and one of the humans roughly patted Asper down. He found the pistol, of course. But nothing else.

The human handed Asper's gun to the dwarf, who looked it over.

"Nice little number," she said. "You'll probably get it back, but you can understand why I'm going to hold on to it for now."

Asper nodded again, silently concentrating on making the dwarf stop talking. *Let's get this over with.* Thieves could be so tiresome.

"*Shield and Spear*," xe said. "Authorize the dwarf as pilot. No restrictions."

ACKNOWLEDGED, the AI said. The entire conversation was pointless; the *Shield and Spear* really didn't have any mechanisms to lock out unwanted pilots— or, at least, didn't have any that were operative once you were *inside* the ship. But the boat *did* know enough to agree with that statement whenever it was made. It tended to make things move more smoothly.

This wasn't the first time in recent weeks that Asper's ship had been boarded.

*   *   *

Apparently believing Asper disarmed and harmless, the two humans moved xir to their ship and locked xir in a small sleeping berth. Asper folded xir legs and meditated, focusing carefully on passing sensations from the ship. It was possible with enough practice and enough sensitivity to the universe to tell when a ship changed directions and even to get a vague sense of velocity, and Asper's senses were sharp indeed. They were near enough to the pirates' base that the ship did not go into tunnelspace to get there, and the flight was exactly 28 minutes and 14 seconds in duration. They were brought in by tractor beam— Asper felt the slight tremor when the beam grabbed the ship— so they were flying into something mobile, not landing on a stationary, ground- or orbit-based structure.

Asper allowed xirself a smile. This continued to go well.

They made xir wait another half-hour before there was a knock at the door. It slid open to reveal the same two humans who had brought xir in.

"They're ready for you," one of them said. "You gonna get up?" He looked as if he was hoping for trouble. Asper looked both of them over carefully before standing up in one fluid motion.

"Who are *they*?" xe asked.

"You'll see," the larger of the two men said, reaching for xir.

"That won't be necessary," Asper said, putting a bit of weight into xir tone. The man hesitated, then let his arm fall to his side.

"Let's go, then," he said, and the two of them turned and stalked off.

Asper narrowed xir eyes and concentrated, expanding xir consciousness to fill the entire ship. By the second turn the elf was reasonably certain of the model and manufacturer. It was a Karem Industries heavy freighter, only lightly customized. A ship of this size was built to move short-range fighters from system to system. There was plenty of room for cargo and personnel, and the ship itself was reasonably fast and mobile for its bulk. Most of the modifications were to add weaponry; the ship was considerably more dangerous than a heavy freighter generally needed to be. It was a good choice for a floating pirate base.

By the time they arrived at the bridge, Asper knew nearly every detail of the ship's construction. With that came the knowledge of the fastest ways to escape the ship, the best places to hide, and the simplest way to completely disable the frigate if it became necessary.

Asper hoped it would not become necessary.

The bridge of a Karem Industries heavy freighter spanned the entire width of the front of the ship. It seemed like poor design; no bridge should need to be any larger than the captain's voice could project, but virtually every station that needed to be staffed by a person was crammed onto the bridge. The captain's chair was the most prominent, of course, with a row of consoles sunk into the floor facing the broad windows at the front of the ship and rows of perpendicular stations on either side. Slightly lower than the captain's chairs were the pilot and copilot's seats. This type of freighter did not have a gunner's chair. They were armed, but the armaments were controlled by six different consoles all controlling one portion of the outside of the ship.

The humans stopped a few meters from the captain's chair.

"We've brought the elf," the larger one said.

"I am aware," a voice said from the chair, which slowly rotated around. "I heard you coming."

Well.

This was unexpected.

*   *   *

Sitting in the captain's chair was the largest dwarf Asper had ever seen. Even more surprising, it was a *male.* Dwarven society was famously and rigidly matriarchal, and while there were plenty of rogue males who had escaped one way or another from a life of near-slavery with their families, for one to have risen to a position of authority *over female dwarves* was rare enough that Asper had never encountered it. Further, most male dwarves were thinner and shorter than females; a life of poor nutrition and hard work stunted their growth and marked them for life even if they escaped. This dwarf did not seem to have that problem. He was seated, but he looked to be at least Asper's height, and easily twice as broad. His beard was glossy black in color, and spilled over an ample gut. This dwarf had been *well* fed.

And then there were the horns.

Grey in color, covered with a thin layer of fur, the horns erupted from at least five points on the dwarf's head to twine together and broaden outward in a halo over his head. They added at least half a meter to his height, and reached out to nearly the width of his shoulders.

How does he SLEEP with those, Asper had time to think, and then the dwarf was talking.

"I am Sulkar Nuh," he said. "All that was yours is now mine."

"That remains to be seen," Asper replied.

Sulkar Nuh laughed, a deep, rolling laughter that would have been infectious under happier circumstances. "This is not a negotiation, elf! I am Sulkar Nuh. I am the Horned Dwarf. I am the Malevolence. And I tell you that your ship and your person are now mine. This is no debate. The only question is whether you survive to fly again or not."

"You claim the Malevolence, then?"

"I do," Sulkar Nuh said.

"The Malevolence is mine," Asper said. "I am Asper, descendant of Overmorrow. I lead the Noble Opposition. Your acts of piracy under a stolen name have ended, Sulkar Nuh."

The dwarf smiled sardonically for a moment, then made a nearly-imperceptible nod to the two humans. Asper moved before they did, crushing one's knee with a swift kick then rolling behind the other and looping a hidden microfilament wire around his neck.

"Do *you* claim the Malevolence?" xe said to xir captive. "Swear allegiance, and serve me. Deny it, and lose your head now."

"Fuck you," he said.

Asper shrugged, flipping a switch that instantly retracted the wire into the two handles. Blood gouted from the stump of the man's neck, coating Asper and much of the bridge between xir and the captain's chair. Screams echoed from every corner of the bridge. Sulkar Nuh was untouched.

Xe dropped the body, letting it thud to the ground.

"*Shield and Spear*," xe said over the comm. "Lock down."

ACKNOWLEDGED, the ship said, putting a number of customized subroutines into effect.

A moment later, there were guns pointed at xir from every corner of the bridge. Sulkar Nuh had not moved, a look of surprised pleasure on his face. The remaining pirate hissed, holding his broken knee and trying not to scream.

Asper stared at Sulkar Nuh.

"Your guns do not frighten me," xe said. "You offered me a choice a moment ago. I offer you one now. You listen, or more blood will be shed. The choice is yours."

Sulkar Nuh's expression did not change. "Stand down," he said, and his crew reluctantly put their weapons away.

"I have heard that Overmorrow died," the dwarf said.

"In battle," Asper said. "Against the Benevolence."

"And so your crossing our path was no mistake," Sulkar Nuh said.

"Correct," Asper said. "Overmorrow controlled a small part of the Noble Opposition's forces. We are scattered across known space, and too many are allowed to claim the name *Malevolence*. I intend to change that. My parent held a fighting force together. I intend to build an *army*."

"And you wish for my little gang of pirates to join you," Sulkar Nuh said. "And fight against the Benevolence. I can only assume that our days of raiding trading routes are over."

"Perhaps not," Asper said. "But your skills will be put to use against more … *interesting* targets."

Sulkar Nuh descended the stairs from the captain's chair, crossing through the pool of blood to stand eye-to-eye with Asper. His tangle of horns towered over the elf's head. Asper met his eyes, every muscle in xir body ready for instant movement if needed. Xe was fairly confident that this dwarf could be beaten in a fight, but to do so with everyone on the bridge taking every clear shot they could find at xir would be a bit more challenging than xe was interesting in. Better to retreat quickly and begin taking the ship apart.

Sulkar Nuh stared at xir, his eyes strangely sleepy-looking. Then he laughed again.

"I like you, elf," he said. "We have been plucking ships out of this route for *months* and never once has anyone thought to *threaten* me on my own bridge. You have *balls*. Or … *whatever* it is you have, they're made of steel." He waved a hand vaguely at Asper's crotch and turned to his crew.

"We've got a new job, folks. I think there's more money to be made with Asper than in lurking here much longer. Anyone care to disagree?"

It was as if he'd uttered a code phrase of some kind. The bridge fell silent instantly. No one moved or volunteered to disagree.

"Well said," he replied. He turned to Asper. "Care to have my navigators lay in coordinates? We should speak in private." He began walking off the bridge without waiting for a response. Asper turned and followed him.

"Your navigators will be discovering soon that the *Shield and Spear* has taken control of your ship," Asper said. "And we will be in tunnelspace soon enough." The hacking package was another of Remember's gifts. It didn't allow control of all of the ship's systems, but controlling navigation was often control enough.

Sulkar Nuh's only reaction was a slight raise of his eyebrows.

"You make for a formidable opponent, elf," he said. "I am glad that we do not have to be enemies."

"I'm glad I only had to kill one of your subordinates," Asper replied. "But I am curious: you seem formidable enough. Why give up so easily?"

"In honesty, I have been looking for you," Sulkar Nuh said. "I have heard that there has been a movement to pull the Malevolence into something more cohesive. Your work has not gone unnoticed in that regard. You command, what, perhaps several hundred soldiers now?"

His intel was surprisingly up to date. "Close enough," Asper said.

"Large enough that you will be looking for a deputy," the dwarf said.

Asper laughed. *Of course.* "It had occurred to me. Although the word that I would use would be *general*."

Sulkar Nuh nodded. "Yes," he said. "I accept."

Asper stopped walking. "I did not offer," xe said. "I know *nothing* about you other than that you command these ships."

"I would have thought that *everyone* knew of the

Horned Dwarf," Sulkar Nuh said, his voice growing grandiose again.

"Known space is large," Asper said. "I had not, and the merchant who sent me on this voyage made no mention of any specific pirate, horned or otherwise."

"Soon enough, then," he said. "My name will be known everywhere. Sulkar Nuh, the Horned Dwarf, general of the armies of the Glorious Opposition! I will be as the immortals!"

"*Noble* Opposition," Asper said. "You may as well get the name right."

Sulkar Nuh waved off xir correction. "*My* opposition will be *glorious*. But that is a debate for later. You say you do not know of Sulkar Nuh. What do you wish to know?" The dwarf's eyes practically twinkled. He was obviously enjoying the conversation tremendously. The two of them entered into a common area furnished with tables and low couches. Sulkar Nuh gestured at a knot of crew members sitting around a table and playing cards. They took one look at him and Asper and quickly fled the room.

Asper stared at Sulkar Nuh. The dwarf seemed to radiate jollity and menace in equal amounts. He was a walking contradiction. A walking, *enormous* contradiction.

"Sulkar Nuh is no dwarven name," xe said.

The dwarf roared with laughter again. "Most people ask about the horns," he said. "But you are too smart! You go straight to the real questions, questions of *identity*. Clever."

"And you did not answer," Asper said pointedly.

"I was getting to it," he replied. "My mother was a criminal, exiled from dwarven civilization. I was a natural birth."

Asper barely controlled xir surprise. Dwarven society had almost entirely done away with natural birth. In fact, had Sulkar Nuh not just claimed to have been naturally born, xe would have sworn no dwarf had been pregnant in generations.

"Does the name have a meaning?" xe asked.

"I have no idea," he replied. "But for whatever reason she declined to name me *Peb* or *Xuh* or some other dwarven male name, and we were not remotely of a caste where a highborn name was appropriate for me."

"Whatever reason? She never told you?"

"I killed her on the way out," he said. "It turns out that generations of gestating infants in vats has made dwarves terrible midwives. Even more so when the dwarves are on the run and have little access to useful medical technology."

Asper could not prevent the wince from crossing xir face.

"It wasn't the horns," Sulkar Nuh said. "Those came later. Years later, in fact. But I was as ... *robust* of an infant as I am a grown man. I was raised by a succession of exiled 'uncles' and 'aunts,' most of whom never knew my mother."

"You do not know where they came from?" xe asked.

"I know they make me mighty," he replied. He said it completely seriously. Asper concentrated on the horns, trying to determine if there was anything magical about them. Xe saw nothing. If the horns truly made Sulkar Nuh mighty, they were doing so psychosomatically.

"If you say so," xe said.

"I do," the dwarf answered. "And they will make *you* mighty through me. I wish to halt the Benevolence before they overtake dwarfspace. Because conquering dwarfspace is *my* destiny. I will help you destroy the Benevolence. And then *you* will help *me* destroy the dwarves."

He's a madman, xe thought. *But a damned charismatic one.*

"I agree to *one* war, not two," Asper said. "And you have dwarves under your command. You are the only male I have seen on board, in fact. They agree to this?"

"I don't care if they do," he replied. "But any dwarf who travels with Sulkar Nuh has reasons to wish to smash the matriarchy. We may not all agree on what comes next. But no matter. I will convince you when the time comes. Until then, I will help you to destroy the Benevolence."

"You may wish to notify the crew of your decision," Asper said. "We should be together when it happens."

Sulkar Nuh gestured at his face.

"You may want to clean off all the blood first," he said.

Asper wiped a hand across xir face, momentarily surprised by the gore on xir fingers. Sulkar Nuh was right. Perhaps a shower would be in order. And then, the formidable task of beginning to meld this gang of pirates into xir army.

The Benevolence would hear from them soon enough.

*   *   *

THE CUSTOMER

The casino floor smelled terrible. It had a lot of other things going on too— it was loud, brightly lit, packed with people, more than a little bit disorienting— but mostly it just smelled. The gnome took a deep breath, picking out the scent of seven— no, eight— different kinds of dried plant being smoked in her near vicinity. The eighth was subtle, but there were at least two different varieties of Carolid tobacco being enjoyed out there on the floor somewhere. The crowd was crazily diverse— mostly gnomes, of course, but only barely, and she spotted all of the Known Races plus a few beings of unclear origin in her first lazy glance across the floor. Everyone seemed to be having a good time. She'd been in casinos before where the prevailing mood was a mix of depression and weary acceptance, where even the winners seemed to know that walking out penniless had only been delayed, not prevented. This one, though? The crowd was having a good time. The house was winning, of course. It always did. But the players thought they were getting their money's worth out of their time. And this wasn't even where the high-rollers played. That casino would probably smell better.

She walked past rows of tables where people were playing games involving cards and boards and chits and tokens— some games she knew, some she didn't. Everywhere had their own local specialties, of course, games that weren't played anywhere else. The other side of the casino was all holo and touchscreen games. No living dealers. Those were the ones she wanted.

She chose a machine sized for bigs since there were more of those available and climbed up onto the stool in front of it. She looked it over. A simple random match game, themed after some well-known local entertainment franchise that she didn't recognize. It would do.

She fed a chit into the machine and blinked hard at it, activating a trigger implanted into an eyelid. The trigger brought sensors in her retinas and fingertips online, probing carefully at the machine in front of her, looking for vulnerabilities in the code keeping it running. A thin yellow halo appeared around the machine. It was a signal, one only she could see. She was in.

She kept her first few bets conservative, winning small amounts of money and then deliberately losing it again to make sure everything was working as she thought it would. Only after she was certain did she go for a big win, pulling in what was probably a day's salary for most of the employees at the casino. A chorus of beeps and flashing lights erupted from her machine, a few holographic fireworks exploding over her head for good measure.

Shit. She wasn't interested in drawing a crowd, although only a few looked her way. A couple more of those displays and she'd have onlookers gathered around her, people hoping to pick up some of her luck by osmosis and maybe one or two who thought they could magic it out of her.

If this was the kind of casino she thought it was, though, she wasn't going to have time to have a problem.

Two minutes later, she'd won enough money to run a small city for a week.

Two and a half minutes later, there was another gnome standing directly at her shoulder.

"You're having a remarkable string of luck," the other gnome said.

"I have days like that sometimes," she responded.

"Remarkable enough that the owner would like to congratulate you *personally,*" she said. "She likes to meet all of her best customers."

"I'd love to," she said, smiling brightly. "So, are you just security, or somebody more important than that?" She turned around on the stool, surprised to note that despite being on a stool sized for bigs the other gnome was nearly tall enough to look her in the eyes.

"I run security around here," she said. "Name's Tarrysh. You planning on being trouble?"

"Wasn't planning to, unless you need me to be."

"It's been a long day."

"I don't know if that's a *yes* or a *no.*"

"Let's keep it that way," Tarrysh said. "You coming, or do I need to escort you?"

"I'm coming," she said, moving to eject her credit

chit.

"You'll find it's not in there anymore," Tarrysh said. "Our system is holding onto it, for safekeeping."

"Safekeeping."

"Yep."

She nodded. This was the right kind of casino after all.

"Let's go meet your boss, then."

*   *   *

Surprisingly, no one bothered to hit her on the way to the interrogation room. Tarrysh called it her "accommodations" just before locking her inside, but that was a polite fiction at best, as the room featured a handful of chairs, a metal table, and absolutely nothing else in the way of furnishing. The floor was poured concrete and the walls cheap paneling, probably over some sort of stone or metal. One wall was mirrored, of course. The lighting overhead— *way* overhead; the ceiling seemed higher than it needed to be— was stark white and harsh. It was every interrogation room she'd ever been in, basically. What it *wasn't*, luckily, was a torture chamber: no suspect drains in the corners, no weird stains no one had bothered to clean up or cover. Tarrysh hadn't even bothered to cuff her to anything or pat her down.

Which probably means I've been scanned a dozen different times on the way down here. She wasn't carrying any weapons anyway beyond a simple utility knife that would probably be a bit worse than useless in a fight. She had some personal biotech beyond the hacking package, but nothing dangerous, and she couldn't find any external signals anyway. Not even any comms. The room was shielded. The entire floor probably was.

She pulled two of the chairs together and stretched out on them. She was probably going to be here for a while, and she was either going to be dead very soon or was about as safe as she could possibly be on this planet. There was no reason not to take a nap.

*   *   *

It felt like she slept for perhaps an hour before a change in the room awakened her. There was another gnome sitting across the table from where she'd built her couch— this one a male, dressed expensively but not ostentatiously. He had the look of a businessman, or at least the clothing of one, but there was something harder underneath it.

Tarrysh had called the owner "she," though. *Not the one in charge. But close enough.*

"So," he said.

She sat up, shoving the extra chair to the side. "So," she answered.

"Let's not do the thing where you lie to me a lot before we find out the truth," he said, his voice calm. "I prefer honesty. My name's Brazel. This is my wife's place. Who are you?"

"Aisra," she said.

"Hi, Aisra," Brazel said. "Got a family name?"

"Inhivra'asti," she said.

Brazel nodded. "Good. Starting off with the truth. Mind telling me why you were trying to hack into my wife's machines?"

They knew who she was already. That could be good news or it could be bad.

"Trying?" she said. "I succeeded. If I'd left after the first transaction you'd never have noticed me."

"We noticed you before you came *inside*," Brazel said. "We pinged your tech at the *starport*. We've been watching you ever since waiting for you to *use* it. I'm revising my opinion of your talents downward right now."

"How come it *worked*, then?" she asked. "You found me remotely but couldn't harden your casino tech well enough to keep me out?"

The gnome's eyes flicked behind her for just a split second, barely long enough for her to duck and cover her head. A fist crashed through the table in front of her, nearly breaking it in half. She hit the floor.

Shit. There was a goddamned *halfogre* standing behind her. She hadn't heard him. She hadn't *smelled* him. How the hell had *that* happened?

"Because we don't always like revealing all of our secrets right away," Brazel said, guessing her thoughts.

Fuck this, she thought. She still wasn't chained or cuffed, and she'd fought bigs before. She grabbed the halfogre's ankle, pulling herself close to him, then tried to scramble up his leg and onto his back. She'd choked out plenty of bigs who weren't prepared for this move in the past.

This one … was. The halfogre did *something*, and he did it so fast she barely even knew what was happening, and then suddenly she was being held up over his head and her back was on the *ceiling* and his giant hand was around her neck and between gravity and the hand it was really hard to breathe and the thought *oh, that's why the ceilings are at that height* floated through her head and it was a ridiculous thing to think but maybe that's what your brain does to you when it's dying from lack of oxygen.

"Kcch," she said.

"What's that?" Brazel said. "Grond, you're choking her. Stop that."

The halfogre shifted his grip, and air flooded back into her lungs. It still wasn't *comfortable* by any stretch of the imagination but she was pretty sure that dying in the next two or three minutes wasn't as likely any longer.

"So here's the thing, Aisra," Brazel said. "We know who you are. We know you've gone by the name *Diode* in hacker circles before. We know you've been at least *mostly* retired for a couple of years, and we know that you just tried to steal an *awful* lot of money from us, but you did it in a really stupid and obvious sort of way that makes us wonder if you're just *that rusty* or if you were trying to get our attention on purpose. Any of this sounding good?"

She nodded energetically. Her chest was starting to compress; it was getting hard to breathe again.

"Put her down," Brazel said, and Grond dumped her back into her chair again.

"Now," Brazel said. "I'm going to ask you *why* again. And you're going to do me the honor of giving me a straight answer, or I'm going to let Rhundi in here to talk to you, and you're going to discover that all this time you've been talking to the *good* cops. So. Why were you trying to hack into my wife's machines?"

"Because I need your help," she said.

*   *   *

"*Stealing from me is a very odd way to get my help,*" Rhundi said. Or, at least, Aisra assumed this was Rhundi.

The other gnome and the halfogre had conferred silently for a moment and left the room, returning a few minutes later. Neither of them had spoken. The new gnome had dyed her fur in red stripes and carried herself with enough authority that if she *wasn't* the boss she probably would be soon. Yes, this was Rhundi. It had to be.

"I'm sorry," Aisra said. "Well, no. I'm not. I did what I had to do. And that includes getting caught, although your *good cops* here tell me I got caught maybe later than I should have."

Rhundi sat in the chair across from her and leaned back, one hand on her chin. "I'm going to say *explain* once, and the next time I have to pry I'm going to leave and have my security strip your tech and toss you off the planet," she said.

Aisra nodded. "Okay. Look, have you heard of a guy named Parson? Parson Oterros? He's a gangster. Runs drugs, guns, all sorts of contraband. Slaves, too, I think."

Rhundi nodded. "I'm familiar with his work. Go on."

"He doesn't seem to like you very much," she said. "He's had me hit six other places before he'd let me come after you. I stole enough for him to turn a moon into an interstellar yacht if he wanted to. He said I had to *prove myself* before he'd trust I was smart enough to steal from you."

"You did the Fourth Horizon job," Rhundi said. The Fourth Horizon was a nearby competitor. Or it had been, before Aisra had nearly cleared the place's bank accounts out a year ago. And then wiped out their insurers, just for giggles. "We'd noticed Oterros seemed to be coming into funds from somewhere. Hadn't connected it to you yet."

"Yeah," Aisra said. "That was me. Remote job. I never even set foot in the place. They weren't being careful enough with their data transmission."

"I don't need the details," Rhundi said. It had the sound of a warning. "And that's quite a claim for someone who just got hustled off the floor for trying to pull a jackpot out of one slot machine."

"Like I said, I wanted to get caught," Aisra said. "Parson's watching me, but he's too damn dumb to know *how* I do anything I do. I needed to come inside and then not come out."

She stared at the woman on the other side of the table. "He's got my kids," she said. "I have five. I know where he's keeping them— his security isn't good enough to keep me away— but he doesn't let *me* out that often, and my ship's tracked. I need someone else to go and get them for me while he's distracted. You've got a rep as someone who can be reasoned with. You get my kids back. Maybe wreck Oterros' organization a little bit while you're doing that. I get myself out of there, and I give you *ninety percent* of the money I've stolen over the last year. The stuff I didn't tell him about. Then I make myself and my family scarce, and you never see any of us again."

"I'd be ashamed to ask for help rescuing *my own family,*" Rhundi said.

"Can't really afford pride right now," Aisra answered. "But I can afford money. Are you going to help me? One way, you beat me up and toss me off the planet and then I send you a lot of money once you've finished the job. The other way you beat me up and toss me off the planet and you don't get anything for your troubles. Or you leave me in a cell someplace, Parson hurts my kids, and you don't get anything for your troubles but you've made an enemy of me for life if I ever manage to escape."

"That sounds threatening," Rhundi said.

Aisra shrugged. "You're grown enough to recognize the truth when you see it. Those are your options. I'm hoping you take the one that gets you paid and wipes a competitor off the map."

"Fill my lieutenants in, then," Rhundi said, standing up. "You have any sense of how bad Tarrysh needs to beat you up, or how long we should keep you here before she does?"

"I'm sure we can work something out," Aisra said, heavy relief flooding her. At least part of it was because it would be Tarrysh doing the beating and not the halfogre. She didn't trust him to not accidentally kill her.

*   *   *

She was released a few days later— without a beating, surprisingly, although she'd been given a pill that had triggered bruising and muscle weakness all over her body, so she might as *well* have been beaten up. *Probably full of nanotrackers, too,* she thought, but those would have been unavoidable anyway— after all, there was no way she would have been able to escape Arradon without *eating* anything. She was given a small amount of money and a one-way ticket on public accommodations to a hub planet near where she'd sent Brazel and Grond. Tarrysh handled that part, glowering at her the whole way to the spaceport and coming very close to actually handcuffing her into her seat, then staying nearby and watching while the boat took off. The bastards impounded her ship. ("We'd have done that anyway," Rhundi had told her. "It'd look suspicious if we let you fly your own rig back home. Consider that the first installment on your payment if you like.")

Luckily, they hadn't bothered to dig her tech out of her, settling for deactivating it while she was on Arradon and leaving it to her to work out how to reboot everything, which took her most of the trip. An hour after disembarking she'd robbed half a dozen local establishments of amounts small enough that they'd likely attribute them to minor accounting errors and she was reasonably flush with funds again.

Her comm came back online with a burst of static.

"Where the fuck are you?" Parson said.

"Balsheon," she said. "I screwed up, Parson. You gotta give me another chance."

An ugly laugh in her ear was the only response.

"Stay where you're at, loser. Find a place to hole up. I'm sending some folks to pick you up. You *don't* want them to have a hard time finding you. There will be *consequences*. You understand this, right?"

"I do," she said. "I'll find a place to stay."

"You do that," he said. "Order room service. Don't leave again. You don't go *anywhere* or do *anything* until I let you again, you hear me?"

"I hear you," Aisra said, and Parson dropped the connection. She allowed herself a smile. With a little luck, that would be the last conversation she'd ever have to have with him, if Brazel and Grond were good at their jobs.

She just wished she knew how big of an *if* that actually was.

She thought for a moment, and made a decision.

What the hell. She'd help them out.

*   *   *

Luckily for Aisra, Balsheon was a reasonably well-established and wealthy planet, located conveniently at the nexus of several important trade and travel routes, and the spaceport she'd landed at, a city called Osarron, was nicely equipped to host wealthy travelers who wanted to spend some time with their boots on the ground in something like standard gravity.

She needed a desk console and a solid comm connection, preferably somewhere where the proprietors understood that taking her money meant it was in their best interests to pay no attention to what she was doing. Using her own equipment would have been vastly preferable, but she had enough software packages stored in her own bioware that she'd be able to make do easily enough. And there were places where the name *Diode* still opened some doors.

She found one in an hour. In an hour and fifteen minutes, she'd followed Parson's orders and paid for enough energy drinks and salty snacks to keep her in her room for a few days. In an hour and a half, she was remotely monitoring the compound he was keeping her children in. In two hours, she had nearly full control of the entire place, from the security to the air conditioning to the sewage system. She wasn't sure how she'd use that, but it would be fun coming up with something.

Until then, it was time to wait. She let the sensors in her eyes pipe in the feed from the room her kids were in and settled back, pretending they were together. Her oldest son fidgeted, keeping watch over the girls. She smiled; Darnel had a protective streak a kilometer wide, and was old enough to have figured out something was wrong, if not old enough to have an idea what to do about it. She spent a few minutes thinking about strategy, wondering what Rhundi's henchmen were going to do to get her children away from Parson. Brazel and Grond hadn't seemed like the type to go in half-cocked and guns blazing. She set a few alarms to alert her if any ships requested an approach vector or if there were any security alerts, then relaxed and let herself drift off to sleep. Rhundi's husband and their halfogre just needed to get to Aisra's children before Parson's goons got to her. Then she'd worry about what happened next.

*　　*　　*

The security alarm woke her up after a short nap.

"Time to play," she said, activating her visual feed again. There was a *chance* that the incoming ship wasn't Brazel and Grond, but if Parson needed to be warned about anyone *else* it was probably time to get her family away from him anyway.

"Okay, Darnel," she said. "You got raised right. You're a smart kid. Show me you're paying attention." Her children were all still in the same room. All of them but Darnel were asleep or on their way there.

She began flashing the lights in the room. Darnel sat up and looked around.

She flashed them again. Then the lights in the corridor outside. She had access to a full map of the compound and camera access nearly everywhere. If she could just get him to follow the lights …

He tried the door. Locked.

"Good boy," she said. The lock, luckily, was electromagnetic, not mechanical. She killed the power to it too and watched it slide open.

For a brief moment, she regretted not forcing him to memorize some simple blink codes. This would be a lot easier if she could directly communicate.

Darnel stepped back into the room and looked directly into the camera. She didn't have audio, but *Mom?* was easy enough to lipread.

Two more quick flashes. The girls were waking up. Darnel moved fast, making sure everyone had shoes on and collecting a few possessions from around the room.

"Follow the flashing lights, son," she said, and—

The feed went dead. Not just her visual feed— *everything*. She was completely disconnected. It was as if Parson's entire place had just ceased to exist.

"No way," she muttered to herself. Perhaps she'd given them too much credit. Had Brazel and Grond just blown the entire damn place to bits? She backed out a step, checking her own comm connection. Had the flophouse she was squatting in cut *her* off? She was—

Something exploded a couple of floors below, and the power went out. Then gunfire; what sounded like a powerful projectile weapon and something energy-based.

Well. Suddenly her comm connection didn't matter anymore. One way or another, nearby explosions meant *time to go*.

She didn't have time to wipe the console she'd been using, but the software she'd installed would burn itself out on its own the next time the machine turned on if she wasn't nearby. She looked around hurriedly, not quite panicking yet, but just on the edge of it. Was there anything she needed? No. Time to go.

She almost made it out the door before it slid open, and she was tackled to the ground before she even had time to process who her attacker was.

"Stay down," a voice said. She rolled, trying to throw a punch. It got her nowhere, the other person locking her elbow and putting just enough pressure on her shoulder to keep her from trying again.

"It's Rhundi, *idiot*," the other person said, and the adrenaline fog cleared a bit. "Stay *down*. I *mean it*. I don't think I got all of them, and you rented a room with only one exit. That was *not* a good idea."

"What do I—" she said.

"Hush," Rhundi said, and the pressure on her shoulder abated. Rhundi pressed a gun into her hand and then got off of her, pointing silently at the corner of the room farthest from the door. *Stay down*, she gestured, then held up two fingers, shrugged, and changed it to three.

Parson? she mouthed. Rhundi shook her head no. *My kids?*

A curt gesture and no answer. Aisra swallowed hard, trying not to read anything into Rhundi's response that wasn't supposed to be there.

They're fine. They have to be fine. She just doesn't have time to explain—

Someone kicked the door in, and Aisra fired her gun empty in moments, not sure who she was aiming at or if she was hitting anything at all. If Rhundi was shooting too, she couldn't tell. The door slid back and forth, trying to recess into the wall but no longer able to, the mechanism screeching in protest. She couldn't see anyone or anything through the holes in the door.

"Did I hit—" she said, and this time the door *exploded*, shrapnel peppering her face and shoulders, smoke filling the room. There were more shots, and she felt her ankle burst as she desperately dry-fired her empty pistol toward the door.

And then, quiet. She blinked tears and ash out of her eyes, trying to figure out what was going on, trying to ignore the pain from her ankle. She didn't want to look. It felt *bad*.

"Can you stand?" Rhundi said. Aisra looked up, her vision still blurry. Rhundi didn't look like she had so much as a *scratch* on her.

"I don't know," she answered, trying to get her good leg underneath her. "I can try."

"Parson's people are dealt with," Rhundi said. "But the local authorities are gonna be here in a minute. We need to be gone by then." She hauled Aisra to her feet. To her *foot*; the other one crumpled underneath her, the pain almost making her black out.

"Shit," Rhundi said. "Darsi, make us a hole. Customer is stationary."

Who the hell is Darsi, Aisra thought, and then something slammed through the wall behind her. There was a crash and suddenly the wall was *gone*, bright sunlight shining through the hole. There was a ship floating just beyond the hole. What had been her wall hung from a cable attached to the ship. They'd brought the wall down with a *javelin*.

For a moment, Aisra was impressed enough that she forgot about her ankle.

"Get the bay doors open," Rhundi said, obviously over comm. "I'm carrying her over. Get as close as you can. We don't have Grond around to just toss her to you." Without another word, she unceremoniously hauled Aisra off the floor, balancing her in a dead carry across her back.

"If I drop you, try to roll toward the boat," she said, and then took a running leap into open air. Aisra had just enough time to scream in terror before they hit the deck, Rhundi not even losing her balance as she carried Aisra toward the med bay. At least, she *hoped* that's where they were going.

"Get moving," Rhundi yelled into the comm. "I'm heading toward the cockpit."

Oh. Well, at least she got to come along for the ride.

A moment later, the ship bucked and she hit the floor, a loud crash sounding from outside.

"What the hell was that?" she asked Rhundi, who was climbing to her feet herself, a trickle of blood dripping from her nose.

"DARSI!" Rhundi bellowed, loudly enough that the comm was probably unnecessary. "Did you just forget to *drop that fucking piece of wall?*"

"Sorry, Mom," a voice said over the shipwide comm. "Maybe get up here and yell at me later? I could use a copilot and maybe a gunner."

It's her daughter. She actually brought her own daughter out here.

"Come on," Rhundi said, pulling Aisra to her feet again. "We're not done with this yet." She half-assisted, half-carried Aisra to the cockpit, her shattered ankle leaving a trail of blood behind them. There were four seats in the cockpit, three sized for gnomes and one much, *much* too big. Rhundi dumped her into one in the back and yanked a medkit off the wall, tossing it to her.

"Fix your foot," she said. "Do the best you can. Then get the console in front of you up and running. We're gonna try to get out of here without any more bloodshed but I may need you to shoot somebody down. You ever been a gunner before?"

"I've never killed anyone before," Aisra answered.

"Until today, I guess."

"You didn't even *shoot* anybody today. Your aim is terrible. But let's not celebrate yet. Hurry up." She turned to her daughter, who looked to Aisra's eyes to not be much older than her son— and therefore not *nearly* old enough to be flying the ship. Aisra decided to do what she was told and buckled herself into the seat, then cracked the medkit open and wrapped the pack inside it around her ankle. The pain lessened immediately. She felt the boat accelerate as she was pushed back into her seat slightly.

"You ready?" Rhundi said. "We're being followed. You don't need to blow anybody up but making them keep their distance is probably a good idea. Our boat's faster, we'll outrun 'em in a minute."

"How do I—" she started to ask, and then the controls in front of her reconfigured themselves into a gunnery interface. There were three smaller skiffs chasing them. She picked the first one and fired a few tentative shots at it. One of them lit up their shields; the others missed.

"Maybe coulda not shot *first*," Rhundi said, as the other two skiffs opened fire on them.

"I thought that's what you *wanted!*" Aisra yelled, starting to panic.

"I just said *make them keep their distance,*" Rhundi snapped. "Not the same thing!"

"Both of you shut up," Darsi said, and they accelerated out of Balsheon's atmosphere. Aisra fired a few more shots toward the skiffs, coming nowhere near any of them. One of them fired what looked like a missile. Laserfire lanced out from the ship and blew it to pieces before it got too close.

"I didn't do that," Aisra said. "Did you do that?"

"Yeah," Rhundi said. "I'm not sitting here doing *nothing*, y'know." Then, to her daughter: "We're set on tunnelspace. Jump when you're ready."

Aisra's entire body shimmered, and the viewscreen in front of her blanked out as the ship jumped.

*   *   *

"So ... what now?" Aisra asked a few minutes later. Darsi and Rhundi had busied themselves with the boat since jumping to tunnelspace, and neither of them had spoken to her.

"We're on the way," Rhundi said. "There was a bit of a setback. Parson may be a bit smarter than you'd given him credit for. By the time Grond and Brazel got to him he'd split, and we're pretty sure the mercs he sent after you *weren't* supposed to bring you back home. They're running him to ground but they don't have him just yet." There was just the faintest edge of derision in her voice.

Aisra took a moment to try and slow her racing heart. "Please tell me my kids are OK," she said, just on the border of tears. *I will not cry in front of her. I won't.*

"We think so," Rhundi said. "Brazel said he thinks Parson will keep everyone safe and alive until he's certain they won't provide him with any more leverage. They're fine so long as they can do him some good."

"I had a feed into his base," Aisra said. "I was watching them. My son. I woke up and everything was cut. What happened?"

"Like I said, he seems to have been on to you," Rhundi said. "A backdoor into your backdoor, or something. I don't know, I don't speak hacker."

Darsi started laughing.

Rhundi shot her daughter a glare. "Not a word out of you, child, I don't care how I phrased it."

"I'm glad you two can *laugh* about this," Aisra said. "I'm paying you. A *lot*. I expect you to take it seriously."

The glare faded from Rhundi's face, and suddenly she was all business again. "And we are," she said. "Like I said, my people are finding them right now. And my daughter and I raced out here to save *you*. Which you should consider being at least a *little* grateful for. In the meantime, check your bank accounts. You should probably make sure you still *have* that money that you're planning on paying us with."

Shit. If Parson was on to her, he could have cleaned her out by now. She hooked into Rhundi's boat's comm connection and checked. About half of her accounts were gone— alarming, but not insurmountable.

"Give me a few minutes," she said, and worked on saving the rest of her money. There would always be time to steal more, if she needed to. She just needed enough right now to show Rhundi—

Oh.

"Change of plans. I was going to pay you 90% of what I've stolen. Parson's found some of my accounts, it looks like. I'm transferring *everything* I have left into a holding account for you."

"What are you going to live on?" Darsi asked.

"I'll be fine," she said. "Money's easy."

"Maybe you *should* speak hacker, Mom," Darsi said. "I've never heard *you* call money easy."

"There's all sorts of things you've never heard me say," Rhundi said. "I'm thinking about saying *several* of them right now. Find your father and get a status report out of him."

"He's ignoring subcomms," Darsi said. "I tried a few minutes ago. They might be out of range, though. Want me to try to get ahold of the *Nameless?*"

"That'd be the next step, yes," she said.

"You heard them, Bellie," Darsi said. "Find the *Nameless.*"

OPENING A COMM, the boat said.

"Bellie?"

"The *Bellicose Witness,*" Darsi said. "I dunno who named him. But I kinda like the nickname."

"A little busy over here, dear," a voice said over the comm. Aisra recognized it. It was Brazel.

"What's going on?" Rhundi asked. "I'd think you wouldn't answer if you were getting shot at."

"We're getting shot at," Brazel said. "But not very well. You have the hacker with you?"

"I'm here," Aisra said.

"If your son survives the next half hour we're going to hire him," Brazel said. "But somebody probably ought to convince him to stop shooting at us when we're trying to rescue him."

"*Darnel* is shooting at you?" The boy had flown before, but she'd never let him near anything with guns on it.

"Um … a bit?" Brazel said. "And some others? He doesn't seem to know who he's shooting at."

"How many other ships are there?"

"Haven't had time to count, dear!" Brazel shouted, suddenly sounding quite a bit more frazzled. "The boy escaped on his own right before we got here, and since then we've all been shooting at each other! Kind of trying to keep us and him alive right now, and he hasn't noticed! Mind if we comm you back?"

"Shoot everybody you're supposed to and get back to me," Rhundi said. "Ten minutes enough time?"

"Oughtta be," Brazel said. "Right back."

He cut the connection.

"Did he say my son *escaped on his own?*" Aisra said. "As in, *stole a ship?* Are the rest of my kids with him?" The mix of parental pride and utter horror she was experiencing was something she was certain she'd never felt before. Usually the two didn't go together like this. She stood up, pacing haltingly around the ship's small cockpit, trying to ignore the shooting pains in her ankle.

"You heard everything we did," Rhundi said. "Might be that boy deserves more credit than he's been getting. If Brazel's right I really *will* hire him."

Aisra nodded, leaning against a bulkhead and trying not to think too hard.

It'll be okay. Everything's going to be fine. Darnel's a good kid. They won't shoot him down. They won't.

The next fifteen minutes were the longest of her life. She tried to open comm channels to each of her children, without any luck— their comms had all been physically disabled by Parson when he took her family. A software block she'd have been able to find a way around, but there was nothing she could do with a broken comm. If Darnel had thought to steal one, he hadn't bothered to contact his mother yet.

The one thing she refused to do was ask Rhundi or her daughter to open a comm back up to Brazel. Darsi looked on the verge of offering a time or two— the girl kept making fleeting eye contact with her and then finding something, *anything* else to look at anywhere in the room— but Rhundi was as calm as could be imagined. She set a course for the boat (back to Arradon,

Aisra assumed) and left the cockpit as the *Bellicose Witness* soared through tunnelspace. Everyone acted like waiting around to find out if their loved ones had survived a space battle was entirely routine.

Aisra laughed, surprising herself. It probably *was* entirely routine. And Rhundi had near-perfect confidence in her husband and his halfogre partner. Darsi did too, for that matter. The girl seemed a bit stressed out, but that was on Aisra's behalf, not her own.

I do not lead the same kind of life as these people, she thought.

And then a ping, and her son's voice over the *Nameless*' comm.

"Mom? Is that you?"

"It's me," she said, relief flooding through her. "Is everyone okay?"

"We're fine," he said. "Everyone's fine. We got away."

"Are you safe? Where are you?"

"The halfogre says he knows you. I'm hoping he's telling me the truth, because otherwise we're captured again. They took out our engines and he boarded. I'd be more worried but I figure most kidnappers don't put you on a comm and tell you to call your mother?"

Aisra broke into tears and started laughing at the same time. "That's Grond," she said. "He's a friend. Tell everyone to do what he says. Where are your brothers and sisters?"

A chorus of shouts and cheers, as the younger kids all weighed in. Aisra glanced at Darsi, who had a broad smile on her face, with just a trace of tears in her eyes as well.

"Do what they say," she said to them. "They'll get

you home."

Grond cut in. "We'll put the kids somewhere they can sleep and get them something to eat," he said. "We need to talk about Parson."

"What about him?" she asked.

"Just a minute," he said, and the connection briefly went dead. When it came back again Aisra couldn't hear her children any more. Grond had either sent them from the room or left himself.

"Rhundi there?" he asked.

"I'm listening," she said. She hadn't returned to the cockpit, so she must have been listening to their conversation from a different part of the ship.

"He's gone," Grond said. "Parson, I mean. The kid's got great timing— he got him and his sisters out just as we were getting into the system, and when we took a few shots at the base it went up like the Benevolence had bombed it. We're gonna debrief the boy to figure out exactly what he did, but I'm assuming no one thinks *laced the place with explosives* is anything on the list, right?"

"Right," Aisra said, rather shaken by the idea.

"Okay. Then Parson's covering his tracks, and didn't want us following him. I think he figured out fast that you'd flown the coop, Aisra, and decided to cut his losses rather than risk Braze and I coming after him. He dispatched a few of his people to try and either shoot us down or the kids, and got out some other way. Point is, he's in the wind somewhere. What do you want us to do, boss?"

"Bring the kids back," Rhundi said. "Don't waste any more time on Parson. I've got somebody else in mind for that job."

"Got it," Grond said, and dropped the connection.

Rhundi walked back into the cockpit. "This is the part where you say *who else did you have in mind* to me," she said.

"Me, I'm assuming," Aisra said.

"Yep," Rhundi said. "Your first job is to find him. Your second job is to ruin the fucker, any means necessary short of hiring someone to murder him, and only because *I'll* handle that part if it comes to it. Your budget is whatever you can steal from him along the way. Get started."

"And my kids?"

"We'll find you a suite," Rhundi said. "Or move you offplanet, whatever you'd prefer. Although I think your son impressed my husband. You may want to stick around and see if we can find something for *him* to do, too."

"I'll talk it over with him," Aisra answered.

"You do that," Rhundi said. "Until then? Get to work."

"You got it, boss," Aisra said. Parson had likely disabled her access to his systems, and was probably hiding his funds as fast as he could. Well, good. She liked a challenge, and *revenge* made for a pretty decent job description.

*   *   *

THE URSINE ABDUCTION

The apartment smelled good. That was about the only thing it had going for it.

Gnomes had an exceptionally good sense of smell. This planet, mostly inhabited by humans, was full of plant life that wasn't pretty enough to be used ornamentally by the locals, but smelled absolutely wonderful to Brazel. Otherwise, the apartment was damp, dark, and far too hot for anyone with fur to ever be comfortable.

But it was cheap. And *cheap* was about the best Brazel could afford right now. Every scrap of funds he made was going toward a rather large debt he owed. And every scrap of funds he made and could *hide* was going toward buying a ship that could get him the hell off of this planet without having to pay any more of that debt.

It was a delicate balancing act, especially since most of his jobs were coming from the person he owed the money to. And he suspected *that* guy hadn't been keeping very accurate books.

Brazel took a deep breath and dropped his bag on the floor. The bag contained a number of important tools: lockpicks, both physical and digital, a hand console with a suite of hacking programs, and a small number of easily-concealable weapons. He preferred to avoid violence whenever possible— on a planet where nearly everyone was half a meter or more taller than you, it was the most intelligent policy— but the world didn't always conform to his *policies*.

His stomach was grumbling. He thought about it and couldn't remember the last time he'd brought any food into the apartment. Hopefully there was something *somewhere*. Now that he was home, hot and unpleasant or not, the impetus to not leave again was damn near overwhelming.

There was a note on the table in his kitchen.

There hadn't been a note on the table when he left. There hadn't been *anything* on the table when he left.

That was bad.

He froze, breathing deeply and listening carefully. The apartment didn't smell like anything other than pora plants and gnome. If there'd been any humans in the room, they'd have left some traces somewhere, wouldn't they?

The only thing he could hear was his heart hammering. And then he caught it— a hint of perfume. A *very* subtle hint. The wearer had bathed a time or two since wearing it, and hadn't been wearing very much to begin with.

And then he recognized the scent, and a broad smile crossed his face. Dropping any pretense of caution, he crossed the apartment and picked up the note from the table.

There were just two words— "Goblin's Thumb"— and a time written on the note. Underneath them, the letter R.

Brazel smiled. The time was two and a half hours away.

Just enough time to get cleaned up and decide what to wear.

*   *   *

The Goblin's Thumb was a local bar, famous— or at least *known*— for one thing, and one thing only: a massive jug of what was presumably some sort of liquor kept in a place of pride behind the bar, prominently featuring a severed goblin's thumb at the bottom of the jug. Brazel had been there a few times and had seen shots served from the jug— the owner of the bar was an ogre and easily able to handle the thing, which was nearly as big as Brazel was— but the level of the liquid in it never seemed to go down. Brazel suspected that the staff was in the habit of simply pouring off any alcohol left in cups around the bar into the jug every night, assuming that anyone willing to drink anything seasoned with the body parts of a sentient being probably had an iron constitution to go with their disgusting taste in liquor.

Under ordinary circumstances, Brazel wouldn't be seen dead in the place. Ogre bars weren't his favorite to begin with, and this one was less hygienic than most, even though the clientele was nearly all human. He'd have to wash his clothes more than once to get the smell out.

But a chance to meet up with Rhundi was worth it. She'd broken into his apartment without leaving a trace— he'd checked every entrance to the place and hadn't seen so much as a scratch that wasn't there before— and there had to be a good reason for it. She could have just commed him, right? She had his frequency. This was practically *flirting*.

He'd chosen his clothes carefully: not his best outfit, which she'd seen before anyway, but still something first-tier, still as close to in-style as he was able to afford, and in damn near perfect shape. He'd had to mend most of his clothes at some time or another. Not these. He'd lost a bit of weight since he bought them, what with most of his spare money funding debt instead of food, but everything still fit well enough.

He was still overdressed for the bar, though.

The place went quiet for a moment when he walked in, but only for a moment, and then went back to normal as everyone there either recognized him or decided he wasn't a threat. His eyes adjusted quickly to the dark. If he knew Rhundi, she wasn't there yet. She was going to make him wait for her.

"This way," a voice behind him said.

Behind him and *above* him.

Way above him.

The ogre standing behind him was young, but had enough scars for any two or three seasoned warriors already. He was thinner than most of the ogres Brazel had met before— he looked positively *unhealthy*, at that— but he carried an aura of menace about him nonetheless.

Brazel spent a moment wishing he'd brought at least *one* gun, and then realized that it probably wouldn't help him too much against an angry ogre. Nobody would use an ogre as a messenger; this guy had to be hired muscle.

He'd been waiting right by the front door to the bar for Brazel to walk in. Brazel hadn't even noticed him. *That takes some talent*, he thought.

"Am I in trouble?" he asked. "Didn't see any signs on the door that the bar was just for bigs."

The ogre laughed, a deep rumble that actually sounded pretty genuine.

"Nah," he said. "Boss said to come find you and bring you to her. She got one of the back rooms. Said it smelled too bad in here." He took a deep breath. "I dunno what she's talking about. Smells fine to me."

"Let's go, then," Brazel answered. "Lead the way."

The ogre shrugged and walked toward the private rooms in the back. There were three on the ground floor and another three on a second-floor balcony. The ogre headed for the stairs and knocked on the middle door on the upper balcony.

"Come on in," Rhundi said from inside. He opened the door, moving himself out of the way so that Brazel could walk past him. She was sitting behind a table— gnome-sized, surprisingly— piled with enough food for three or four people. Two of the chairs around it were sized for bigs. Rhundi nodded at Brazel, then looked up at the ogre.

"Thanks, Grond," she said. "Go have a few drinks. You'll know if I need you."

The ogre nodded and slipped noiselessly out of the room.

"Didn't know you were hiring ogres for muscle," Brazel said. "Didn't know you were hiring muscle at all, actually."

Rhundi laughed. "Be glad Grond didn't hear you say that. He's a halfogre. Make sure you find out the difference before you talk to him again."

Brazel had heard of halfogres, but didn't know

anything about them. "That something to be proud of?"

"More like something to not screw up," Rhundi said. "He's kinda particular about it at the moment."

"Mind if I eat?" Brazel asked. "I was actually hoping this was a date. The table's set for a meeting."

"Yeah," Rhundi said. "I've got a proposition for you. The others will be here in a bit. I wanted to sound you out about it first."

"So long as I don't have to wait to eat," Brazel said.

"For the food, no. For the date? I imagine so," she said.

A dozen responses crawled through Brazel's head and he rejected them all, choosing instead to tuck into the food. Rhundi sat silently for a moment, then laughed.

"Clients will be here in a minute," she said. "They told me they needed two people for the job, and that it wasn't going to be good for bigs. That means Grond's out. So I thought I'd throw you the chance for a side job that pays better than the mess you're in now. I assume you're all right with the idea."

Brazel nodded, his mouth full of pastry. The faster he got his debts paid off, the better.

*   *   *

A few mouthfuls later, the clients were there anyway: a pair of olive-skinned, dark-haired human women who perched at the edges of their seats like they were afraid of contracting a disease and gave no indication of even thinking about touching the food. One was dressed like she came from money. The other, much younger, was wearing a nondescript brown blouse and pants and had the look of a servant. Grond let them into the room, nodded wordlessly at Rhundi, then shut the door on his way out. Brazel listened for the halfogre's heavy

footsteps as he walked away from the door and didn't
hear them. He was staying close during the meeting.

Brazel didn't speak either, assuming that if Rhundi
wanted him to be part of the negotiation— or whatever
this was— she'd let him know. He kept eating. The four
of them sat in awkward silence for a few moments and
then the older woman tapped the other on the shoulder
and began communicating with her in rapid sign
language.

"Madam Veldt wishes to make something clear
before we proceed," the attendant said. "She can both
hear and understand you. She does not speak but that
does not make her deaf. You will speak to her, not to me.
Do you understand?"

"We understand," Rhundi said, and Brazel nodded.
Madam Veldt gestured to her attendant and the girl
produced a datapad from somewhere under her clothes
and handed it to Rhundi. She began signing again.

"This is your contract," the attendant said. "You are
to break into a certain home and remove a certain item
from the library. Once you have removed the item, you
are to take it somewhere no closer than five light-years
from this location and then destroy it, as completely as
you are able. The datapad also contains detailed maps
and schematics of the home and the neighborhood
surrounding it."

"This is Madam Veldt's home," Rhundi said. Madam
Veldt's hands stopped moving, a clear expression of her
shock.

"What?" Rhundi asked. "You didn't think I was
going to meet with you without figuring out who you
were first, did you?"

The old woman sneered and began signing again.
"The home is not *precisely* hers," the attendant said. "It
belongs to her husband. They are … estranged." Madam

Veldt seemed to disagree with this word and began signing directly to her attendant, and the two of them directed their communication at each other for a moment.

"Estranged," the attendant said. "Madam Veldt is not welcome in the building where the item resides, and is physically unable to enter the library. Thus her preference for bringing in a third party."

Brazel couldn't resist. "Physically unable to enter the room? Is she married to a gnome?"

"She is," the attendant confirmed. Brazel's mouth dropped open. This job had just gotten a *lot* more interesting. He'd never heard of any such thing. He found that he had quite a few questions.

Rhundi shot him a look. "Physically unable? The room's built for us, then?"

Veldt and the attendant exchanged a look. "There may be more to it than that," the attendant said, and Brazel noticed something interesting: the girl was talking on her own now, not waiting for her mistress to sign a response. Madam Veldt, in fact, suddenly looked quite depressed. "The room *is* sized for gnomes, but Madam Veldt is not an especially large woman. Any door too small for her to enter through would necessarily be rather uncomfortable for gnomes as well. She is *literally* unable to enter the room. The mere thought has been known to produce rather violent nausea."

Madam Veldt *was*, in fact, starting to look rather green. She put a hand on her attendant's knee, then made a curt gesture with her other hand that Brazel had no trouble interpreting. It meant *wrap it up*.

"How's that work?" Rhundi said.

"We do not know," the attendant said, again without waiting for Veldt to answer the question.

"If there's magic involved, the price is going up," Rhundi said.

"You will find yourself well-compensated," the attendant said pointedly. "For one so focused on research, it is surprising that you have yet to finish reading the contract."

"And I suppose you've got some way of knowing how far away we are when we destroy the item," Rhundi said. "Speaking of, you haven't told us *what it is* yet."

Madam Veldt began signing again.

"We do not," the attendant said. "But Madam Veldt is concerned that her *husband* may. The library, and the item itself, has immense value to him."

"Again with the word *item.*"

Madam Veldt paused and took a deep breath, then responded.

"It is a stuffed animal," the attendant said. "Specifically, a large, meat-eating quadruped common to human worlds known as a *bear.*"

Brazel decided the best thing for him to do was to continue eating without making any comments. Rhundi managed to keep a straight face, a ripple in her fur the only sign of her reaction to their target.

"You want us to steal a stuffed bear. From a library, in your house. And blow it up," she said.

Madam Veldt nodded.

"And you want us to be *far away* when we blow it up. We can't just blow it up on-site. Or set it on fire."

The attendant began translating again. "Madam Veldt believes there may be one or more tracking devices embedded in the bear. Her desire is that her husband remain permanently uncertain as to whether it still exists or not. The hope is that you will be out of range of any method he might use to track his possessions when you destroy it."

"And if we aren't?" Rhundi asked.

"There are provisions in the contract that will be

activated if you do not survive an attempt to recapture the bear," the attendant deadpanned. Brazel coughed, a morsel of meat suddenly stuck in his throat.

"And if we have to kill him to get away with it?" Rhundi asked.

"In extremis, you are to destroy the bear on site, then escape by any means short of killing Madam Veldt's husband," the attendant translated. "If he dies, your contract is void."

"Of course it is," Rhundi said, making eye contact with Brazel.

Who, for his part, had rarely been happier. This job looked like it was going to take a few days at a minimum. That was *much* better than a date.

*   *   *

Madam Veldt's contract didn't specify a time frame, so they spent a full five days on surveillance and planning before taking any action. Veldt's home— her husband's, at least— was in an older section of town, a neighborhood that once was the crown jewel of the area but had started to trend toward run down and abandoned in the last decade or so. Most conveniently, the building next door was unoccupied. Rhundi had a dozen nanocloud cameras keeping tabs on the property at all times, and she and Brazel took turns keeping physical eyes on the place as well. Grond stayed in the abandoned house full-time, providing a second set of eyes and trailing Veldt's husband whenever he left the house. Conveniently, the gnome— Paschal was his name— seemed to have a steady job and left the house on a predictable schedule.

"I don't think we can make this much more straightforward," Rhundi said, reviewing their plans.

"There's mechanical locks on just about all the entry points on the house. The house is old-school enough that it's almost totally analog on the outside. There's some 'bot presence on the inside— Veldt says they have a lot of servants— but nothing electronic at all keeping the place locked up. So we get in through this window—" she indicated a ground-floor window in the back of the house on the blueprints that Veldt had provided them, the closest entry point to the library— "and we go to the library. If we get spotted by one of the 'bots, we disable it as quietly as we can. We steal the bear. We go out the same way we came in. If that's blocked, we go out the back door. If that's blocked, the front. Worst-case scenario, the library's got a skylight, but we'll have to shoot it out and then climb up to it so it's going to be really noisy."

"And then Grond picks us up," Brazel said.

"And then Grond picks us up," Rhundi repeated. "He'll monitor from the ship, a few minutes out. There's a spot nearby for him to pick us up if we need him to, otherwise we get out of the neighborhood first and meet him somewhere less likely to get noticed. We hop over to the next system and drop the bear into a star and collect our money. Any questions?"

"Not a thing," Brazel said, pointedly avoiding saying the words *This looks easy*, or anything else that might turn their luck against them. It *did* look easy— a simple theft; he did a job like this nearly every week— but he knew better than to say so out loud.

*   *   *

They broke in in the morning, opting to make their move when the house was empty and risk being seen going into the house rather than caught inside it. Brazel came prepared to pick any lock he'd ever encountered and nearly dropped his tools laughing when he discovered their chosen entry point had been left unlocked. It took just a few moments to shove a screen out of place and then they were inside. The window opened into the end of a simple corridor, the floor covered in shabby carpet. Two doors on the left led to bedrooms, according to the floor plan, and a pair of double doors at the end of the corridor led to the library. The walls featured framed artwork, with vases and other decorative items scattered on narrow tables on either side of the corridor. Everything was sized for gnomes; a human would have been quite uncomfortable in this part of the house.

Rhundi took a deep breath. "Do you smell something odd?" she said.

Brazel inhaled too.

"Plaster," he said. "Fresh plaster. Where's that coming from?"

"The ceiling," Rhundi said after a moment. "Look. They've lowered the ceiling recently. Why the hell would they do that?"

Brazel looked up. Rhundi was right; the ceiling was distinctly lower than it ought to be even in a gnome-sized home, and what's more, it was clearly *new*. The walls had been white at one point but years of neglect had yellowed them somewhat. The ceiling was a flawlessly clean white.

"Look," he said, pointing. "Panels. Three of them." There were three square panels, perhaps a meter to a side, spaced evenly down the corridor. "What do you think those are for?"

"Decorative?" Rhundi said.

"Doesn't match anything," Brazel said. "Doesn't really *add* anything. Maybe, but only if Paschal is a *terrible* decorator. Let's keep going."

"Anything not matching the blueprints we got makes me nervous," Rhundi said.

"We can cut out right now," Brazel said. "Window's right there. All we lost is some time."

Rhundi stood still, thinking.

"Nah," she said. "I just don't like unknowns. Let's get the bear and get out of here."

*   *   *

The library was locked, but Brazel had them inside in moments. The room was the first genuinely impressive thing either of them had seen since entering the house; the room was round, bookshelves ringing the entire outer edge. There were two balcony levels above the ground floor, with an enormous skylight taking up most of the ceiling. Across from the entry doors was a fireplace, with three overstuffed chairs, all sized for bigs, sitting in front of it. In the center of the room, a silver orb sat atop a pedestal.

Rhundi whistled. "Grond's gonna be *so pissed* that he missed this."

Brazel was incredulous. "He *reads?*"

"We'd never get him out of here," Rhundi said. "Where's the bear?"

"I don't know," Brazel said, walking further into the room. "What's the— oh."

"Oh?"

"I think I found the bear," he said, pointing at one of the chairs.

Rhundi walked around the chair. She'd found a picture of a bear while researching the job, and this … *thing* looked at least *mostly* like one of those? It was a shocking turquoise in color, with stubby arms and legs, and a *much* friendlier look than the actual bears she'd seen, which sported sharp teeth and long claws. The expression on its face *might* have been meant to be a smile. Its eyes were a shiny dark blue, with a vaguely surprised look painted onto them.

It sat perched in the center chair, facing the fireplace. The chair faced away from the door, so it hadn't been visible until they came all the way into the room.

It was twice as big as either of them. It was almost as big as *Grond.*

"That's not gonna fit out the window," Brazel said. "Was I the only one picturing something we could *carry*?"

"You'd think Veldt would have *mentioned* this little detail," Rhundi said, clearly infuriated.

"Maybe she didn't know," Brazel said. "She *did* say she wasn't able to get into the room. And, speaking of that, do we think this has anything to do with it?" He pointed at the orb. "I think it's buzzing."

"That's alarming," Rhundi said. She waved a hand over the orb, coming close but not quite touching it. "Any idea what this is? You're right, it's vibrating. And … do you hear that?"

Brazel listened carefully. The orb was emitting a low moan, just at the edge of what he was able to perceive.

"You think humans can hear that?" he said.

"No idea," she answered. "But I know I don't like it. Maybe it would be a lot worse if we were human, who knows. You think this was what was keeping her out?"

"Best guess," he said. "So how do we get the bear out of here?"

"We take it through a door," she said. "No choice. We're not going to be able to get it out of a window and neither of us can get it through the skylight. So we go out the back door, nice and quiet, and we're gonna have to risk Grond popping into the neighborhood to get us. We head straight out of the atmosphere and hit tunnelspace the second we can and we're back planetside in a few days. By the time anyone's noticed we're here and figured out it's a problem, we're already gone."

"Works for me," Brazel said. "Let's see how heavy this thing is. It's stuffed. It can't be *that* heavy."

He pulled the bear out of the chair, and the alarms started.

"Oh, *fuck*," he said.

*   *   *

"A pressure sensor. He put a pressure sensor *underneath the* bear," Rhundi shouted, clearly in disbelief. "Who the hell *does* that?" The alarms were deafening, almost certainly audible from outside the house, and Brazel could barely hear her. She opened up a comm to Grond.

"Get here!" she shouted, then spent a moment trying to hear the halfogre's response and dropped the connection. *If he heard the alarm, he'll figure it out,* Brazel thought. He grabbed the bear by a leg and started pulling. It was *much* heavier than he'd expected. He gestured and Rhundi grabbed another leg. They dragged the bear to the door, which Brazel threw open, and got it halfway into the hallway before the panels in the ceiling slid open and the shooting started. Brazel dove to the right, upending a table and hiding behind it, and Rhundi threw herself underneath the bear. The three ceiling guns kept up a steady stream of blue energy, mostly concentrated at the table Brazel was hiding underneath.

"Stun blasts!" Rhundi shouted. "Or they'd be through the table by now!" Indeed, the energy didn't seem to be causing any damage to any of the objects it was hitting. Brazel's foot was slightly exposed for a moment and went numb as the energy washed over it.

"How the hell come they're focusing on *me*?" he
shouted. "You're the one with the bear! Shouldn't they
be shooting *you*?" Indeed, Brazel was taking the vast
majority of the shots, and those directed toward Rhundi
were … *missing.* By rather a *lot.* Brazel had nowhere to
go; if the energy didn't stop he was going to be pinned
underneath the table until the authorities came.

Rhundi thought quickly and then smiled to herself as
a solution came to her. She pulled a knife from her belt
and opened the seam up the bear's back. A few moments
of frantically pulling stuffing out from inside the bear left
just enough room for a gnome to crawl inside. She rolled
over twice, managing to position the cut seam right next
to where Brazel was pinned down.

"The guns aren't shooting at the bear!" she shouted.
"The trackers must be keeping them away! Get in here!"

Brazel wriggled his way inside the bear and ended up
facing Rhundi, each of them with one leg inside each of
the bear's legs. The hammerpulse sound of the guns …
stopped.

"Unbelievable," Brazel said. "He's got the guns
programmed so they can't fire on the bear. I did *not* think
this was how today was going to go.

Rhundi ignored him, opening a comm. "Grond, you
there? That window we got into the house through?
Blow us a hole we can walk out of. We're inside the
bear." She listened for a moment. "Yes, *inside* the bear.
Quit fucking laughing and do what I'm telling you!"

There was a muffled explosion a few moments later.

"I doubt he got the guns," Rhundi said. "We need to
figure out how to stand up and walk this thing out of the
hole Grond just opened up. You up to it?"

"I can't feel my right foot," Brazel said. "That might
make it a bit more difficult."

"Push through, dear," she said, and the two of them wrenched the bear into what was probably pretty close to a standing position.

"You don't happen to remember which way the window was?" Brazel said.

"This is ridiculous," Rhundi said, and pulled the seam a bit wider so that they could see. The air was full of smoke and haze and the one gun she could still see, the one furthest away, was still trained directly on them. They'd dropped down from the ceiling through the square tiles, and the way the gun moved around as if trying to position itself for a clear shot was genuinely creepy.

"You didn't bring a gun, did you?" she said.

"One in my waistband and another at my ankle," he said. "I think you can reach the one at my waist. I barely have the room."

She reached around his back, patted him down, and discovered a small projectile gun under his waistband at the small of his back.

"Start walking backwards," she said, and reached past his head to take aim at the furthest of the three guns. Two shots brought it crashing down from its cubbyhole.

"The angles are no good for the other two," she said. "But I think if we can get to the hole in the wall we ought to be all right. How long has it been since we set off the alarm?"

"Can't be more than a couple of minutes," Brazel said, trying his best to walk on his numbed foot. "The nearest constabulary was, what, ten minutes away?"

"So we figure we've got no more than three or four minutes," she said. She reopened the comm. "Grond, the *second* you see a flash of blue coming out that hole in the wall you snatch us up and get us on board. *Yes*, that means I'm letting you pick me up. *Yes we are both in the bear.*"

"That's it," she said to Brazel; Grond was laughing so hard that Brazel could hear it over her private comm. "I am *not* paying him for this job. He's getting his money's worth just out of mocking us."

They only fell twice on the way to the hole Grond had blasted in the side of the house. True to his orders, the halfogre was on top of them the moment he could see them, blowing the other two guns to bits and quickly getting them inside their boat afterwards. He let the two of them struggle out of the bear on their own, opting to head for the cockpit and get them into space as quickly as possible.

"We will never speak of this again," Rhundi said, brushing cotton fibers off her shoulders.

"I think Grond's never going to let us *forget*," Brazel said.

"Not a chance," the halfogre said over the comm. "Get up here. We're being chased."

"Must have taken longer to walk down the hallway than I thought," Rhundi said, heading for the cockpit. "How good of a shot are you?"

"I can manage," Brazel said.

"Take the belly gun, then," she said, pointing the way. "I'll go copilot with Grond. Good luck."

*   *   *

Rhundi was comming him again before he'd even managed to find his way into the belly gun. "There's some legit local authority back there," she said. "And one or two ships that look like private security. Right now we're focusing on getting away. Don't kill anyone unless you have to. They're not shooting—"

Her transmission was cut off by the sound of laser fire richocheting off the shields. The boat rocked, Brazel nearly losing his footing as he scrambled into the belly gun.

"Are you about to say *never mind?"* he shouted over the comm.

"Shoot the blue ones!" she said. "Those are the private security. The locals are already falling back."

"Already?"

"Probably called off by the mercs," she said. "We're going to be out of their jurisdiction pretty soon anyway. This boat's faster than you think. Keep us alive while Grond and I outrun them."

Brazel dropped into his seat, which adjusted to his size and strapped him in automatically. *Luxurious*, he had time to think, and then the outer hull of the boat went transparent and combat diagnostics started popping up over anything the AI thought might be a plausible target. There weren't just "one or two" private security skiffs chasing them, there were *four*, two just barely entering sensor range and two that were actively firing on them.

"Don't kill anybody, she says," Brazel muttered as he opened fire. "Come *on*." It was much harder to shoot at someone if you *didn't* want to kill them. That usually meant taking out engines rather than, say, the cockpit, or blowing a wing off, and then hoping that you just *disabled* the engine rather than making it explode. And in this case, they were being *chased*, so the engines were on the *wrong side* of the boats he was shooting at. He settled for spraying fire at whatever mercenaries were closest, trying to disrupt their attack patterns and keep them on their toes. The shields on the lead ship were overloaded quickly, and a few more shots blew a small hole in the port side. *That'll do*, he thought. With no shields and an inconvenient hole leaking vital atmosphere that one was probably out of the fight. He briefly lost sight of the other lead skiff as Grond threw them into a

spin, then got lucky— *or not, maybe?*— and clipped a
wing, sending another of their attackers into a tailspin of
their own.

Hopefully she can still land that thing, he thought.
The other two were far enough out that a missile lock was
possible but laser fire would be wasted. He locked on to
both but didn't fire, hoping that the sirens in their ears
screeching about the lock would be enough to convince
the mercenaries to break off the assault.

And then he had no more time to think about it, as
Grond dropped the boat into tunnelspace and their
pursuers went away. The hull went opaque again—
watching as you sped through tunnelspace was pretty for
a moment or two, but then tended to produce excruciating
headaches— and Brazel unstrapped himself from the
belly gun and climbed back out. It was *possible* for
someone to follow them, with a bit of luck and some
good guesses, but boat-to-boat combat couldn't happen in
tunnelspace unless both boats jumped on the same vector
and at the exact same time. For the moment, they were
safe.

*   *   *

"Nice flying," Brazel said to Grond upon finding the
halfogre in the cockpit. He shrugged.

"All I had to do was outrun some locals. I feel like
we got off pretty easy," he said. "We've had more trouble
stealing less stuff in the past."

"You think they let us go?"

"Nah," Grond said, relaxing back into his seat. "I
think Paschal genuinely thought anybody trying to steal
the bear would be caught in the house. The security he
hired was supposed to detain a couple of amateur thieves,
not win a dogfight. Once you took the first one down the

fight went out of the rest of them awful quick."

"Let's make sure we aren't being tracked," Rhundi said. "We're supposed to fire that stupid bear into a star, so I don't think anyone's going to be upset if we tear it apart first. You got a course set?"

"Yeah," the halfogre said. "Dropping out of tunnelspace six times at random intervals to change direction. We'll end up plenty far away, and the only way anybody's gonna catch up to us is if they drop a blockship on our flight path. It'll be a couple hours before the first drop-and-spin. We've got time to take your bear apart."

He grinned, an evil glint in his eyes. "Or sew him back up again, if you want to keep him. I mean, the three of you have such a *history* together and all. I'm sure your kids will love him."

Brazel, deciding not to respond, decided he was glad that gnomes were too furry to blush. Rhundi shot Grond a dirty look and left the cockpit.

Grond waited for a moment longer.

"Oh, go ahead and follow her," he said.

Brazel scurried out of the cockpit.

*   *   *

Rhundi was merrily tearing the bear apart by the time he found her. There was actually tiny tufts of cotton— or whatever it was the bear was filled with— floating in the air in a gauzy cloud around her.

"Scanned it for nanocams," she said over her shoulder. "Nothing. Can't find anything hidden in the stuffing. I'll give you two guesses where the trackers are."

"Eyes?"

"Eyes," she said. She tossed one of them to him. There was a thin wire, probably some sort of antenna, poking out of the back of it. "They're both live. Transmitting right now, although the signal's not going to get anywhere so long as we're in tunnelspace. Veldt was right. He not only put his bear on a pressure sensor, and wired his house to *protect* it, he replaced both of its eyes with transmitters."

"Are you starting to wonder if we'd get more money by *giving it back* than we are for stealing it?" Brazel asked. "This thing's clearly *really* important to Paschal. Maybe he wants it back more than his wife wants to hurt him by stealing it."

Rhundi thought about it for a moment. "I have a better idea," she said. "How long do you think it'll take to clone the signal these things are sending?"

"I could probably pull it off, yeah," he said. "Couple of hours, with the right electronics. Which I'm guessing you don't have on the ship?"

"No," she said. "Do you need to physically have the transmitters to copy the signal?"

"Now that we know they're transmitting? No," he said. "They're just sending a signal that says *I'm here*, basically, right?"

"I imagine," she said. "It's a repeating signal. He just needs a receiver tuned to it."

"Yeah, I can pull that off," Brazel said. "Just need the hardware."

"Okay," Rhundi answered. "We're gonna destroy these two, just like we said we would. But we're gonna keep the bear. And we're making half a dozen or so more transmitters. We decide we need some money down the road, we strap a pair of them onto a drone ship and see what happens next."

"You're saying *we*," Brazel said.

She looked him over. "Yeah," she said. "I am. You do good work. Is there a problem I need to know about?"

"Not a bit," Brazel said, suddenly feeling warmer. One more source of income was great. His debts paid off, a new boat free and clear … and Rhundi.

Maybe he'd eventually get that date after all.

*   *   *

REBIRTH

The universe blazes white.

The light is everything, and bores into his brain like a physical force. He tries to fight it, to cover his eyes, to hide from the shining. Nothing changes.

I can't move.

There is nothing but the light. No sound, no sensation at all other than pressure from the whiteness. He tries to move his arms again, to blink, *anything* to stop the light for a moment. Nothing happens. There is only the light, for what seems like forever.

And then it stops, and there is only darkness.

*   *   *

After a while — it could have been hours or decades — he decides that he is dead. Death, it turns out, is terrifically boring. The light has lasted ten minutes, or a thousand millennia, and now it is gone, replaced by nothing at all. This isn't what death is supposed to be like. Death is supposed to be reward, or punishment, or at least *oblivion*. This is none of that. Only consciousness, and darkness. There isn't even any pain, now that the light is gone. He finds that he misses the pain. It was proof that he is real.

*   *   *

For the next million years, he tries to scream.

*   *   *

When the voice finally comes, he can barely hear it. It begins as whispers, indistinct mumblings that just fail to resolve themselves into words he can understand. There is one speaker, then dozens, then hundreds, then a single voice again. He strains to hear, to understand, his ears not up to the task by the slightest of margins.

"Who are you?" he tries to ask, and makes no sound.

OUR NAME IS PATIENCE, the voice replies, and he finally understands. Had he the power to do so, he would weep with relief.

"Where am I?" he asks. NOWHERE, Patience replies. NOT YET. WE ARE DECIDING IF THERE IS SOMETHING TO BE DONE WITH THEE. THOU HAST SINNED AGAINST US, YOUNG ONE, AND SINNED GRAVELY. BUT WE HAVE BEEN KNOWN TO FORGIVE.

"I don't understand," he replies, and still his words make no sound.

UNDERSTANDING SHALL BE GRANTED TO

THEE WHEN WE WISH IT, Patience replies. AND NOT UNTIL.

He thinks carefully, or tries to. He does not remember his sin. A spike of fear shoots through him as he realizes just how little he *does* remember. He is unable to recall his own name, or his mother's face. Perhaps he deserves what Patience is doing to him.

"Why can't I see you?" he asks.

SOON, Patience says.

*   *   *

Another eternity passes, and the light returns. With it is Patience's voice, still and quiet, everywhere and nowhere at the same time.

THY VISION SHALL BE RESTORED TO THEE, Patience says. DO NOT TRY TO UNDERSTAND WHAT THOU ART SHOWN. TRUST IN US THAT ALL SHALL BE MADE WHOLE SOON.

"My sin," he says. "Have you forgiven me? What did I do?"

THOU ART FORGIVEN, Patience says, AT LEAST FOR NOW. BE CALM, AND BE THOU RENEWED.

And he remembers. A warship, stolen. A dash across space, thoughts of revenge burning in his soul. And an attack upon a capital ship larger than any he had ever seen before. And after that ...

death

... he cannot remember. A burst of heat and flame, and shattering cold, and ignominy.

I was dead I was dead I died I was killed I DIED
THOU DIDST NOT DIE, Patience says.
I died I was shot and burned and crushed and blown

to pieces I died

NO, Patience says.

my body gone my spirit scattered nothing left no breath no hope no light no love no worries no fears died died died died DIED

BUT THOU ART ALIVE, Patience says, AND WE HAVE FORGIVEN THEE FOR THY TRESPASSES AGAINST US.

"Who am I?" he asks again.

REMEMBER.

"I died," Haakoro says, as his name is restored to him. The world returns.

*   *   *

Patience— it could only be Patience— stands before him. Xe *looks* like an elf, but Haakoro can't recall ever seeing an elf that looks like this one before. Patience's face is a black so deep it borders on obsidian, and xe stands nearly as tall as an ogre. Xe is wearing plush, soft robes— the word *raiment* floats through Haakoro's head unbidden— of the deepest blue he's ever seen. Xir hands, as pure white as xir face is black, are folded atop a needle-thin cane that Haakoro suspects xe has never actually needed. The look on xir face radiates wisdom and ...

Benevolence.

As that word echoes through his mind Haakoro finds himself more afraid than he has ever been. He was filled with rage before; rage at tyranny, rage at being manipulated, rage at war and at death. Now he only feels fear.

"Speak," Patience says. Xir voice is soft, pleasant.

"Thou hast questions. Ask them."

For a sudden, terrible moment, Haakoro wants to apologize. To throw himself at Patience's feet and beg xir forgiveness. He doesn't move. He's not sure he can yet.

"How?" is all he asks. His voice ... it isn't his, and it sounds tinny, as if it was coming out of a cheap speaker. His sight is restored, but he still can't feel any of his body. But he's definitely *hearing* now, instead of having Patience's voice suddenly appear in his head. That's progress, of a sort.

Patience smiles, and something about the kindly look on xir face reminds Haakoro of his grandparents. The thought repulses him.

"Oh, Haakoro," Patience says. "Thou came to us with anger in thy heart, and with murder in thy soul. Thou brought war to our home, to our *Testament*. And we defended ourselves, did we not? We did. And thy hurts were turned away, and thy weapons rendered irrelevant. But *thou?* Thou did *not* die. And we *found* thee, and brought thee close, to our bosom, for we ... well, we found thee *interesting*, and we brought thee back to wakefulness, even as we seek now to restore thy body and thy movement to you."

For the first time in a while, Haakoro really *tries* to move. His body is entirely inert; he can't even *see* himself. His arms and legs respond to no commands. He screams again, a sound of frustration and fear, and Patience *tsks* at him and something happens and he can't even hear himself any longer.

"Sleep now," Patience says. "We shall see thee again soon, and we shall discuss thy future. But thou should not try to move. We have much to do, ere thine movement be restored along with thine sight and speech. Witness." Patience steps back from Haakoro and, almost lazily, waves a hand in front of him. The air solidifies, becomes reflective. And Haakoro sees something in that reflection, something that makes the screaming begin again, and this time he is unable to stop.

He sees a single eye, floating in a glass tube, suspended in a pink-tinged liquid. Other, meaty things, less identifiable, float in the tube with his eye. Wires trail off from the back of the eye, leading *somewhere*. Perhaps his brain is in there somewhere as well. Perhaps he is a machine intelligence of some sort now, a sentient 'bot that only *thinks* of itself as Haakoro. He tries to turn his eye away from the sight of itself. It does not move. The world, blessedly, fades to black anyway.

*   *   *

When he comes to, he is walking. Or perhaps he is being carried. He tries to stop moving and cannot. Two black-armored Benevolence agents walk a few steps in front of him, both carrying frightening-looking assault rifles. There are two more behind him. He is, he realizes, not entirely sure how he knows they are there, but he does, and they are.

As he walks, he tries to test his body, and he finds that he can *feel* it, but he cannot control it. He feels the floor on his feet and the slight breeze as the air swirls around him. His arms sway at his sides. There is a slightly bitter, metallic taste in his mouth. He tries to pull his gaze toward his feet, to get a look at himself, to no avail. The agents do not speak. They lead him to a doorway and they stop. So does he.

A few moments of silence, and then the doorway slides open.

And behind the door, infinity.

Haakoro enters.

*   *   *

The door opens into what appears to be the outer hull of the ship. But this can't be true. There was no airlock, no screaming wind as the inner atmosphere of the ship voids itself into empty space. There has to be *something* keeping air near him— a transparent dome, perhaps. Is he breathing? He thinks he is. No way to breathe in outer space.

In the distance, Patience stands alone, leaning on xir cane, xir blue raiment and white hands glowing against the black. Patience raises a hand and beckons Haakoro toward xir. Haakoro approaches. He thinks he is doing it on his own, but he isn't sure.

"Beautiful, is it not?" Patience says.

Haakoro finds that he can control his neck. He looks upwards. Patience is right; the stars, undimmed by even the slightest hint of atmospheric haze, are indeed beautiful.

"They are," he replies.

"It belongs to us," Patience says. "All of it."

"Must be nice," says Haakoro. "I didn't even own the ship I was using."

Patience smiles, brushes the back of xir hand across Haakoro's face, or whatever it is that is underneath his eyes now. The gesture is almost tender.

"Thou art so young," xe says. "Fine. For the sake of clarity: it belongs to *me*. It is *mine*. The entire expanse of the sky, and all the stars, and all the galaxies, and all the planets and all the beings and all the lives within. We— *I*— rule it all. Alone."

Haakoro would raise an eyebrow, but he's not sure he has any muscles in his face. He wonders if this is braggadocio or ignorance. Surely Patience *knows* that there are wide swaths of space that the Benevolence does not yet occupy.

"Dost thou know where we find our warriors, young man?" Patience asks. "Our agents of Benevolence?"

"I don't," he answers. It's never occurred to him to wonder. He has always assumed that they were volunteers at first, or perhaps conscripts, but surely no conscript would act as single-mindedly as the Benevolence does. Surely volunteers, and volunteers with a long, arduous training process.

"We have chosen that word for a reason," Patience says. "Our agents do not come to us. Some try, surely; they are allowed into our service in other ways. No, our agents are *found*. Some of them are identified as early as their first year of life. Others come to us in their adolescence. And some ... well, some elude us for a longer time. But they are *found*, young Haakoro, and they are brought into the fold, all of them, and once they are here they serve us well."

"How do you find them?"

"Their abilities call to us," Patience says, closing xir eyes and letting xir head drift backward. Xe waves xir arms in an oddly ethereal gesture; Haakoro cannot feel the breeze that must be animating the sleeves of xir garment, for them to wave so. "Hast thou not felt *different*, Haakoro, for all of thine life? Hast thou not felt the very *universe* responding to thy needs, putting that which thou needed in front of thee at the very moment it was most needed? Didst thou not *survive* in the blackness of deep space, thy body and life-support shredded, thy very being scattered to the stars? Thou art *extraordinary*, Haakoro. And we have need for the extraordinary. And we require thy service."

He is suddenly certain that he has blood, for it has gone cold. Freezing, in fact. He's being *recruited*.

Patience locks eyes with him. Xe knows that he understands, now.

"Look upon thy body," xe says, and mirrors the air again. And for the second time Haakoro is certain that he has no interest in seeing what Patience wants him to see. And, for the second time, he is unable to resist.

Most of his body is mechanical now. Some parts appear to be growing new skin; he can see into his own chest cavity, where his heart beats and his lungs expand and deflate, but his ribs are gone. His chest cavity is enclosed in black metal, with patches of skin spreading like mold across concrete. The parts of him that are not mechanical, that are not *growing*, are encased in armor.

Benevolence armor.

His left arm, his right hand— he thinks it is flesh under that gauntlet, attached to the rest of him via synthetics. His lower body appears mostly intact. His face is a horror. One eye remains; the other is a glowing light. There is flesh where his nose and mouth should be, but they are simply *gone*, a mass of scar tissue where facial features used to be. A smooth piece of black material— it might be fabric— encases his scalp and comes down over where his ears might be. A sound escapes him involuntarily, and he realizes with a jolt that something is speaking for him. His mouthless face cannot produce speech any longer. Something, built into him somewhere, is synthesizing his thoughts into words.

"Let me die," he says. "Please." He concentrates his entire will, and manages to force his body to its knees.

Patience reaches out and caresses his forehead again.

"We have a gift for you," she says. "If thou wishes to die, thou has but to make the choice. And if thou wishes to live, thou must make that choice as well."

"What is it?" he asks.

Patience moves to the side. Behind xir, in the distance, is a pedestal.

Atop the pedestal is a helmet.

"Choose," Patience says. "But choose wisely, and choose ... *rapidly*. The door will open to thee, if that is thy wish."

Xe walks past him, striding to the door, which slides open to admit xir. Haakoro feels full control over his body restored to him. He stands, looking around. *A choice? What choice?*

Right then is when all the air goes away. And a moment later, the heat.

There never was any atmosphere out here, Haakoro realizes. *Patience was keeping me alive.*

He can feel his exposed flesh starting to freeze, and his lungs begin to crumple in his chest as what little air was in them is forced out. His internal organs are exposed to the cold. The helmet is only a few yards away. That has to be the choice Patience referred to. He can put on the helmet— he can *join the Benevolence*— or he can die here, alone and unheralded, a speck on the hull of the largest ship in the galaxy.

I can't do this, he thinks, and he steps toward the helmet anyway.

I don't want to die.

He has to, he thinks. He *cannot* become one of them. Death is *better* than this alternative. Joining the Benevolence would be betraying everything he ever wanted, everything he ever was, every person he ever met.

What did they ever do for you, part of him says. *Patience offers you power. Who ever took you seriously, Haakoro?*

"Xe called me extraordinary," Haakoro says, and his hands trace the surface of the helmet. Starbursts explode in his vision as the liquid in his eye begins to freeze. He can feel himself slipping away; one way or another, he only has another few moments. All he has to do is *not do anything*, and this can be over. All he has to do is make the right choice.

Haakoro makes his decision. The helmet clicks into place over his head, and the last thing he feels before losing consciousness is the needles snaking their way into his brain.

*   *   *

THANK YOU

... for reading *Tales from the Benevolence Archives*. Reviews are absolutely critical to gaining visibility for independent authors, so if you enjoyed the book (or even if you didn't!) please consider reviewing it at the book site of your choice.

And Amazon. Please, God, review it at Amazon too.

ABOUT THE AUTHOR

Luther M. Siler was born in 1976 and currently resides in northern Indiana. Sharing his house with him are his wife, son and an assortment of pets. He has a job, but it's not as interesting as it used to be and it's probably different now anyway.

His other works include two other *Benevolence Archives* novels, the near-future *Skylights* series, a nonfiction book about teaching called *Searching for Malumba*, and a collection of short stories, *Balremesh and other stories*.

You can follow Luther at his blog at http://www.infinitefreetime.com, or on Twitter at @nfinitefreetime.

ALSO BY LUTHER M. SILER

THE BENEVOLENCE ARCHIVES, VOL. 1:

Troll evictions! Dwarf pirates! Daring rescues! Angry gods! Impossible technology! Oversized bars! Pissed-off ogres! Disrespectful spaceships! All this and a mild disregard for proper wound treatment!

THE BENEVOLENCE ARCHIVES, VOL. 1 is a novella-length collection of six short stories set in a common universe. Combining elements of space opera-style science fiction and high fantasy, THE

BENEVOLENCE ARCHIVES tell the adventures of Brazel, Rhundi, and Grond, a gnome/halfogre team of smugglers.

THE PLANET IT'S FARTHEST FROM: A simple job in a saloon goes poorly for Brazel.
THE CLOSET: Brazel and Grond are hired to teach someone why gambling can be a bad idea.
YANK: Dwarven pirates. 'Nuff said.
REMEMBER: Brazel and Grond are hired by one of the galaxy's most powerful people for a suspiciously easy job.
THE CONTRACT: Rhundi tries to get through a simple business negotiation without anyone being shot.
THE SIGIL: Brazel and Grond encounter something horrifying on a frozen rock in the middle of nowhere.

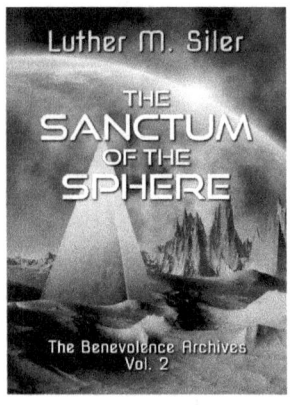

THE BENEVOLENCE ARCHIVES, VOL. 2: THE SANCTUM OF THE SPHERE

"Go rob that train." Nice, normal. An everyday heist.

But nothing is ever normal for Brazel, Grond and Rhundi.

A simple act of motorized larceny quickly explodes into a galaxy-spanning adventure for the two thieves. Blade-wielding elves, a fast-moving global war, a secret outlaw space city, incomprehensible insectoids and one impossibly lucky human are just the start of their problems. And that's before they learn that someone from Grond's past has gotten the Benevolence involved...

What is happening on the ogrespace moon Khkk?

Who are the Noble Opposition?

And what is the secret of THE SANCTUM OF THE SPHERE?

BALREMESH AND OTHER STORIES

A last stand against ultimate evil. A refugee from outside of time. A corrupt governor and a graveyard of wronged spirits. A technological breakthrough that could change human culture forever, or end it entirely. An executioner listening to a genocidaire's final statement. And a door, hanging in the air, a door that must never be opened. These and other tales await you within BALREMESH AND OTHER STORIES, a novella-sized collection of short stories and microfictions in the horror, science fiction and fantasy genres.

SKYLIGHTS

August 15, 2022: the *Tycho*, the most advanced interplanetary craft ever designed by the human race, launches from Earth on an expedition to Mars. The *Tycho* carries four passengers, soon to be the most famous people in human history.

February 19, 2023: The *Tycho* loses all communication with Earth while orbiting Mars. After weeks of determined attempts to reestablish contact, the

Tycho is declared lost.

2027: Journalist Gabriel Southern receives a message from a mysterious caller: "Mars." Ezekiel ben Zahav isn't talking, but he wants Southern to accompany him for something— and he's dangling enough money under his nose to make any amount of hardship worth it.

SKYLIGHTS is the story of the second human expedition to Mars. Their mission: to find out what happened to the first.

Read on for an excerpt: the prologue to SKYLIGHTS.

Flashbulb memory, they call it. It's when you remember exactly where you were when you first discovered something or saw something happen.

If you're younger than me, which a lot of you probably are, then your first flashbulb memory is probably related to terrorism somehow. Anybody in, say, their early thirties or older probably remembers exactly where they were on September 11, 2001. A little younger than that and your first flashbulb memory is probably one of the bombings in Chicago in 2018.

I was six years old when the space shuttle *Challenger* exploded. It was January 29, 1986, at exactly eleven thirty-nine in the morning. I was in first grade. For some reason— I could look this up if I wanted, I suppose, but my first-grade self didn't know, so I'm not going to bother— NASA had decided that it would be great if they put a schoolteacher on the Space Shuttle. Her name was Christa McAuliffe, and she'd been a middle school teacher, her students not a lot older than I was at the time.

There was a ton of publicity about her presence on the shuttle. Come to think of it, that might have been the reason that NASA put her there in the first place. Every single kid in my school was watching the flight launch on television. The *Challenger* took off, and we all clapped. Seventy-three seconds later, an O-ring failed on the shuttle's right Solid Rocket Booster. There was a little puff of smoke from the side of the ship.

Some of us were still clapping.

I remember noticing it and wondering, for the split second that I had, what had happened. And then the *Challenger,* with me and millions of other people around the country watching, silently blew apart. There were a few seconds of shocked silence in the room, and then every kid in the class— every one in the building, probably— started crying at once.

You know what? Writing that just now, I wondered what my teacher must have done afterwards. I can't even remember her name. I can remember the wood surface on my desk, because I dug my fingers into it so hard that day that they scratched it and I got splinters. I can remember the wood-grain on the television set they had us watching. I can remember being surprised that Rachel Douglas, the biggest butthead in the entire first grade, was crying as hard as I was. But I can't remember a single thing that our teacher did to try and bring everybody back to sanity after watching that happen. That's how flashbulb memories work; you'll remember the event itself forever, but that doesn't mean you'll remember anything else that happened around it.

Seventeen years and two days later, it happened again. This time, it was the shuttle *Columbia*, and I was twenty-four and no longer sitting in a classroom. In fact, when the *Columbia* was falling apart in the morning sky over Texas, I was stuck in traffic and late to work. I found out about it about ten minutes after I got in, when the smarmy dope from the office next door made some sort of comment about it to me. We had the Internet by then— yes, there was Internet back then, although I think we might have still been calling it the World Wide Web— and I saw the entire thing on CNN's Web site. This time there weren't any tears, just a dull sort of ache in the pit of my stomach. I spent the rest of the day on the computer, chasing down eyewitness reports and trying to devour whatever little bits of actual news managed to leak out. It was funny; I hadn't spent much time thinking about space flight since the first grade, but suddenly the families of the men and women on that shuttle were all I could think about.

I was working for the *Indianapolis Star* at the time, splitting my time between a biweekly column in the science section and general reporting on local news for the rest of the paper. It was a good job; I was happy enough, and making enough money, but I wanted something different from my life.

I decided to write a book.

A year later, I'd completed *Nothing to Bury: the Martyrs of the Space Race*, a look at the lives of the astronauts who had died on the *Challenger* and the *Columbia*, as well as a host of other lives lost in the pursuit of space, and a look at the culture of NASA in between the two disasters. I was pretty proud of it as a piece of work; I wasn't expecting it to necessarily sell well to the general public, but it was a good piece of writing. It did better than I'd expected, enough that I've been able to be comfortable with freelance writing since then. I'm still working for news sites and some of the few print papers that are left, mind you, but I can pick my own assignments and do my own reporting now as opposed to having people assign my projects.

You know where this is going, don't you? I imagine you do.

On August 15, 2022, after years of technical and political delays, the space shuttle *Tycho*, carrying four astronauts, launched on a six-month journey to Mars. They were to remain in orbit around Mars for thirty days, during which they would land on the planet's surface for the first time in human history, then to return to Earth. The run-up to the launch was the biggest public relations bonanza NASA had ever seen. Everything just *stopped* the day the *Tycho* launched. It was just like it had been for the *Challenger,* only times a hundred. They just weren't as good at hype in the eighties, I guess.

I was watching at home, with a couple of friends— I actually had a little party for the launch. I didn't realize how tense I was until I looked at my hands afterwards. There were furrows in my palms from my fingernails. Then the shuttle took off, soaring into a perfectly blue sky, and I held my breath for a few moments.

The launch went off without a hitch, though, and pictures of the *Tycho* blanketed every website and print doc on the planet over the next few days. For the next six months, everyone was obsessed with Mars. The astronauts provided regular updates on what they were doing. You could get daily blink messages from them if you wanted to, and progress along their flight path was updated live on a map running at the top of CNN.com for the entire duration of the trip. Those six months, I'm convinced, inspired a whole generation of new astronauts, astrophysicists, and pilots. I've never in my life seen America more excited about science. It was amazing.

And then, on February 19th, 2023, when the long voyage was finally over, we... well, we don't actually know what happened. The *Tycho* was supposed to aerobrake into orbit around Mars, stay in orbit for a day or two, and then the astronauts were going to leave the ship to descend to the planet's surface in a lander. They were going to stay on the surface for two weeks or so, doing experiments, exploring the Martian surface, and making history.

There wasn't anything resembling photo evidence, not good evidence at least— NASA had been sending a steady diet of pictures and video from cameras affixed to the outside of the *Tycho* for months, but they failed at the same time as the audio feed. But we were getting audio beamed back from inside the cabin. Right up until the point where the flight commander, a decorated Marine pilot by the name of Alondra Gallegos, spoke the last words that the *Tycho* sent back to Earth.

"Is that..." was all she said.

After that, nothing. No sound, no signals, no big explosion to be played on the news over and over again. Just nothing at all, and what started off as mild concern slowly morphed, over the next few days, weeks, months, into the certainty that, somehow, the ship had been lost. There was hope for a while that there had just been some sort of global communications failure, that the *Tycho* was still out there but had lost the ability to talk to us. Sadly, those hopes didn't make much sense in reality— the *Tycho's* communication capabilities were among the simplest systems on the ship, something a talented twelve-year-old would have been able to repair, *and* there was a redundant backup system. Anything catastrophic enough to have completely crippled the ship's ability to talk would have caused fatal damage to the rest of the ship as well. We just couldn't figure out what. Conventional wisdom eventually decided there had been some sort of asteroid or meteorite impact, something like that.

There was no flashbulb moment for the *Tycho*. The families of the four people lost on that mission— Alondra Gallegos, Harrison Brown, Kassius Newsome, and Ai-Li Wu— will never be able to move on. Many of them are convinced that their family members are still out there somewhere. There was no national mourning like there was for the *Challenger* and the *Columbia*. It was as if, after three high-profile ship losses, this time the country just wanted to forget about it.

I got a few calls for interviews after the *Tycho* lost contact, and a few more a few months later, once NASA officially stopped trying to reestablish contact with the ship. I turned them all down, though; I didn't want to base any more of my career on profiting from the deaths of people more heroic and important than I was. I didn't want to write about space any more.

Little did I know.

www.ingramcontent.com/pod-product-compliance
Lightning Source LLC
Chambersburg PA
CBHW070820120626

46556CB00002B/593